*Dedicated to two men who loved the Western Plains of
Nebraska and remembered the West as it once was.*

Charles Hafer: 1889–1982
Donald Hafer: 1913–1997

Secrets of the North Table

by

Alan Hafer

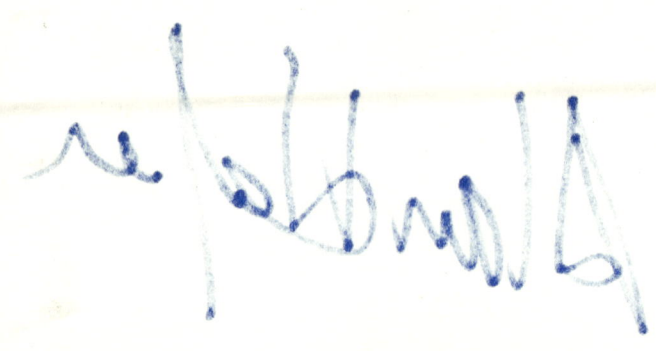

This book is a work of fiction. Any resemblance to actual events or persons, living or dead, is entirely coincidental.

"Secrets of the North Table," by Alan Hafer. ISBN 1-58939-792-4 (softcover); 1-58939-793-2 (hardcover).

Library of Congress information on file with publisher

Manufactured in the United States of America.

CHAPTER ONE

AT LEAST GEORGE ROBERTS AND HIS FAMILY KNEW THEY were coming. Someone had found the courage to leave a note on their wagon when they had been in the small settlement of Medicine Lodge the day before. The Klan was gathering to rid the Nebraska prairie of papists, Mexicans, and the "hermaphroditic abomination to God" living in their house. George's wife Sarah, their son, and the two young Californians were hiding in the root cellar connected to the basement of their two-story frame house. George was sitting in the rocking chair he'd carried onto the buffalo grass, his Winchester lying across his knees.

George had watched their dust for nearly a quarter of an hour. With the temperature over one hundred degrees and not a hint of wind, the brown cloud created by the approaching mob rose straight into the sky. He figured the modern boys in their motorcars would arrive first, followed by men pushing hard on lathered horses. Last to make it to see the spectacle would be wagons hauling the older folks, some even bringing children. 'Probably think its going to be more entertaining than the church socials held nearly every Sunday,' George thought, 'ranking right up there with the Old Settlers Days celebration on Labor Day.

1

'*They'd better hurry, wearing those white sheets, probably crawling with vermin that most of the poor fools took right off their beds and ruined by cutting out eyeholes.*'

The dark blue sky announced a fierce plains thunderstorm was also on its way. He couldn't feel the wind on the ground yet, but swirling clouds to the northwest signaled a storm with wind and lightning, maybe even rain and hail.

Wouldn't it be something if the wind blew out their flaming crosses, or - even better - if a twister carried the lot of them away while his family was safe in the cellar? It made no difference to him! God could blow them away, drown them in a flood, burn them with lightning - or he could ventilate the rib cages of several of his neighbors with his rifle. They shouldn't be doing this, and so help him, if they touched one hair on Sarah's or the boy's head he'd blow them all to hell.

He recognized Schwartz as soon as he rode into view. The self-appointed leader of the newly formed North Table Chapter of the Ku Klux Klan was a German with a poor dirt farm only five miles away - near enough they were always stepping on each other's toes in the wide-open countryside.

"That's close enough! Stop right there, you old chicken thief," George yelled, carefully aiming his rifle. "You don't fool me none - even if you are dressed-up like you were going to marry that ugly daughter of yours off to some drummer. You have no business here. Take this bunch of idiots with you and go back to tending your miserable dirt farm."

"Now George," the heavily accented reply came from the white-cloaked figure taking care not to ride any closer to the house. "We held a meeting at the church and decided them two Pope-worshipping greasers you got living here got to go. Having that girl swishing around and praying to them beads is bad enough, but you got that queer in there and that's going to bring the Lord down on the whole table. They got to go. You got to send 'em back to the Mexican devils that spawned them."

George's shout that the man and his fool followers could go to hell was lost in the din of cheers, shouts, and threats coming from the multitude riding into his yard on lathered horses and creaking wagons. The metallic click of a shell levered into the chamber of the rifle was lost as well.

"What's the matter, you sheep-herding, chicken-stealing cowards?" George yelled. "Did you leave all your fancy automobiles at home, feared I'd recognize who you were? Hell! I was expecting to own some of them contraptions after I killed you. Now you show up on wagons and horses, and I don't know one of you from the other."

A man whose voice he recognized as another neighbor - somebody he'd shared work and hard times with and whose wife had helped in birthing his son - shouted, "Come on George, there's no reason for talk about shooting. We don't mean you no harm, but the Lord will smite us if them sinners stay among us. You know I can't stand to be hailed out again. I've lost my place once to hail, once to a twister, and once to fire. It ain't right. You're taking chances could cause me to lose my place!"

'*And may God protect us from small-minded men who blame all their faults on Him and their friends.*' "Shit, I know you've had troubles, Louie," George yelled back. "But that ain't no call for you to be wearing them sheets and joining with this bunch of lamebrains. These people you threw your lot in with ain't even got the brains to wash them damn sheets before putting 'em over their heads. I'll bet the better parts of most of their stupid kids are in the stains on those rags."

Struggling to maintain leadership, Schwartz yelled above the din, "Don't be talking to good people that way. We've come to carry out the Lord's will. We're going to make this a God-fearing country for you to raise your son in. Someday you'll thank us. Now bring them greasers out, and we'll take them to the depot. A train will come through in the morning to take them back to California."

"Yeah. If that queer one be still alive after we git him. The girl can go, but he needs some lessons first," an anonymous voice called out from the back of the crowd. George saw the confrontation had reached a critical point. He'd been in enough bar fights to know a crowd is a coward, especially a crowd hiding behind stained sheets. He needed to act quickly to take the fight out of them. He sighted his rifle on the water box of the steam car that had just arrived. *'Too bad Johnny Lawrence was the only one with the nerve to drive his car. He sure wasn't going to be driving it home.'*

The heavy bullet tore through the thin metal of the boiler, releasing pent-up steam with a shrill scream, scalding old man Schwartz's prize gelding. When the horse reared in agony, it tore loose from its owner's grip and ran bucking through the crowd. All the other horses panicked, and then stampeded back toward Medicine Lodge. Before the smile had left George's face, the entire crowd was running backward, dodging bucking livestock, and trying to keep their best sheets from dragging in horse dung.

A violent gust of wind blew over the tall wooden cross the sheeted figures had erected on the road and were trying to ignite. George could tell the evening's events were over when the few drops of rain turned into a torrent, and the parched soil quickly became bottomless mud. *'Like a cow pissing on a flat rock.'* "If any of you sumbitches try to get into my barn to get dry, I'll shoot you.

"That'll learn you to come messing around here," he called back as he scrambled through the front door of the house he'd built with his own hands. He watched the departing circus through one of the glass windows the Union Pacific Railroad had transported to Medicine Lodge from the city of North Platte.

Only when the rain was over and the crowd gone did George walk outside to the storm cellar.

Intended to prevent Nebraska weather from harming his family, the three-inch thick doors and mounds of earth had kept Sarah's shrieks from reaching the outside. When George threw open the heavy wooden doors, the pitch and intensity of her screams assaulted his ears. He was sure the unworldly clamor would bring the Klansmen back. After his eyes adjusted to the dark, he saw a scene so horrible he no longer cared about his neighbors wearing sheets.

Soaked with blood and holding his old buffalo-skinning knife, Sarah kneeled over the ripped, gore-covered bodies of the teenagers who had come from California to help care for their son, Donald. The almost seven-year-old boy leaned back against the wall of the cellar staring hypnotically at the grisly scene, his hands over his mouth.

"My God, Sarah! What have you done?" George screamed in anguish. "How could you?" Slumping to his knees in horror, he stared at what his beautiful wife had done to her best friends, the only people on earth except him and the baby that mattered to her.

When his son ran to him and threw his arms around his neck, George picked up the boy and his wife, one under each of his ranch-toughened arms, and hauled them into the house. George placed his son on the floor beside his favorite hand-carved toys. He then sat Sarah on the kitchen table and began scrubbing off the blood, using water he pumped out of the cistern directly into the sink.

As he worked, he realized that most of those sheet-wearing people had visited before just to drink a glass of water drawn inside his house.

When Sarah was clean, he poured half a bottle of whiskey down her throat, stilling her moans with sloshes of the amber liquid. When she passed out, he burned her bloody clothes in the wood stove they used for cooking and heating.

Over the next several days, George made several trips to town to buy all the steel plating and two-by-fours available. When he had gathered enough materials, he built a new roof over the cellar. He left a space only twelve inches high, just enough to cover the bodies of the young people. He covered the steel with a foot of earth, making the tomb level with the ground around the house.

George never forgot the incredible sadness he felt as he placed the bodies in the pit with their favorite silver adornments and then covered their grave with dirt. He lived with vivid memories of cementing closed the passage between the basement and the storm cellar, and he never took pride in the glorious lilacs and rhubarbs that grew over the secret burial site.

For the rest of their lives, neither George nor Sarah ever discussed that terrible night or the two teenagers again. He didn't leave Sarah alone with their son until he was fifteen, heavily muscled, and known around the county as a star athlete who was good with his fists. George never knew why his beautiful wife killed two of the people she had loved most in the world. He blamed it on loneliness, women's complaints, ostracism by his family, and the hardships of life on the prairie.

As the months passed, everyone who lived around Medicine Lodge figured George had finally come to his senses and sent the Mexicans packing - and so much the better. The community accepted them back with open arms, but George never forgave his neighbors or forgot what they had done.

———

George thought a great deal about the events preceding the murders as he grew older. Sarah had been deliriously happy when she had told him about her two missed cycles and that she was going to have his child. They'd danced around the house - she in her lithe, girlish way, and he stumbling along like a big, clumsy oaf.

But depression had come over her quickly. After two months, there had been no more laughter, singing, or smiles - only tears and sadness. When he asked her what was wrong, she'd just say she missed having a female around. A friend she could share secrets with - someone who liked pretty things as much as she did. She had longed desperately to talk to somebody different from the heavy-thighed, ample-bosomed, red-faced, dressed-like-men women of the plains who lived on the isolated table.

It had been his idea to send for one of the females from the ranch where she'd lived. The return telegram from the ranch owner announcing he'd be happy to send Consuelo, a young woman Sarah had always thought of as a little sister, had cured her depression immediately. The stipulation that Jesus, Consuelo's brother, had to come along had been fine, even though George knew it would take their God-fearing neighbors a while to accept the idea that Mexicans named their offspring after the Lord's only Son.

Sarah's spirits had improved after Jesus and Consuelo arrived. She'd acted like her old self again, as she had when she was the happiest, prettiest woman on the table.

Everybody had loved her then, and George's heart had swelled with pride whenever he caught another man casting admiring glances in her direction. She had always been the finest looking woman in western Nebraska, and she married him.

Sarah and Consuelo rekindled their friendship and became closer than sisters. They both fell in love with the plains and spent days exploring the grasslands around the ranch. They packed lunches, had George saddle two horses, and rode out with the wind. When they weren't riding, they were playing with the baby and tending to chores around the place, always in high spirits.

George supposed that was why what happened in the storm cellar that day just never made any sense.

CHAPTER TWO

ADAM ROBERTS DROVE INTO THE YARD. FLASHES OF lightning silhouetted the house against the black summer sky. Gnarled elm trees planted by his grandfather, George Roberts, bent over before the shrieking wind that had knocked out the power lines. Perched on a hill looking over miles of Nebraska prairie, the house appeared before him as it always did in his dreams: stark, foreboding, and framed by a malevolent sky.

After retiring from his position as a history professor at a small college in the suburbs outside Boulder, Colorado, Adam had decided the time had come to face his childhood fears. The heart attack he'd survived a year ago might have signaled an end to his career as a teacher, but it had also forced him to struggle into good physical shape. Now that he was healthier than he had been in twenty years, he had the strength to confront his demons.

On the downhill side of six feet tall, in excellent condition for his sixty years, Adam looked to be anything but a cardiac patient. Even with his hair loss, most people who met him for the first time thought him ten years younger.

Adam's love of history had grown from the stories his grandfather had told him of the Old West. As a boy, he'd heard tales of outlaws, gunfights, and depredations by all manner of men. He supposed it only natural that his grandfather's descriptions of the olden days had always made him feel a little cheated. He should have descended from one of the dangerous characters of the stories. Instead, he came from a long line of farmers. His forebearers had spent their time following mules and riding tractors, unmoved by the great adventures happening just over the next hill.

Adam had tried to live as if he had been one of those fast-shooting, straight-talking knights of the frontier. He had sown his wild oats while chasing adventure as a mountaineer and professional ski patroller in the Colorado Rockies after graduation from college. Then he settled down to raise a family and labored to instill the love of history in future generations.

Dignity, integrity, and honesty. Values learned on the plains served as his life's guideposts. When he died, he wanted his tombstone to read, *He Did His Best.* He had wanted it to say, *He'd Done His Damndest,* but that inscription marked the grave of a ranch hand killed in a gunfight in the trail town of Ogallala, Nebraska, in 1893.

Finally, forty years after he'd left the flatlands of Nebraska, Adam unlocked the padlock on the front door of the deserted farmhouse where he had been raised. He planned to stay there alone until he found out why fears that had caused him terrible agony as a child still tormented his soul.

Adam dropped his suitcase on the kitchen table - the furnishings were the same as they had been before his parents passed away ten years ago. The familiar nausea in the pit of his stomach was close to unbearable. He had lived with that sick feeling since the first time a crazy woman with an upraised knife ran into his room.

He had made the three-hour drive from Boulder to find out whether his lifelong nemesis had been a real ghost or a figment of a child's over-active imagination. Had she been one of the monsters that hid beneath the beds of most young children, or was she something else entirely? If she was a ghost, why had she picked him to torment? None of his brothers, parents, or grandparents had ever seen her.

He yelled up the narrow staircase to the second floor where he had tried to sleep as a child, and where she had tried to kill him nightly. "You still here, you demented old bitch? Or did you finally leave and find some other kid to frighten?"

Adam regretted his boldness immediately. What if he'd made her angry? What if she flew down the stairs to finish him off? Keeping the table between him and the stairs, Adam felt the weight of ambivalence and anxiety he'd carried for more than fifty years.

He knew better than to be afraid. Calling out wasn't going to cause either a ghost or his childhood imagination to kill him. The idea was absurd, but then why was the feeling in the pit of his stomach so strong? Why were his hands shaking? Why did he have an overwhelming desire to run out the still-open door, jump into the sports car he had bought for himself as a reward for surviving the heart attack, and race straight back to the mountains?

Trying to regain his courage, Adam decided to look around the farm before setting up housekeeping. He walked through the trees of the windbreak planted by his grandfather. Except for the elms, there had never been an attempt at landscaping around the house. Water was over four hundred feet below the surface of the earth. His grandfather George had always said they lived closer to hell than water and that hell was probably a lot more refreshing.

Adam's mother had regretted her inability to grow flowers and green grass to make the house look nice instead of stark and dusty. Whether she had his father paint it white, light blue, or emerald green, the house stood out boldly from the sun-baked, dust-covered gold and brown of the prairie, but it had never been pretty.

Adam drew a deep breath and entered his childhood home once again. He walked through the dining room and climbed the stairs to the second floor. The built-up heat under the poorly insulated roof almost forced him back down again. He hurried to throw open the windows to enjoy the strong winds, remembering how miserable most nights in those rooms had been.

As a child, he believed his room was hotter in the summer and colder in the winter than anywhere else on earth. During the winter, glasses of water on the nightstand had frozen so solidly they cracked under the pressure of the expanding ice. Especially cold nights found four boys and two dogs cuddled together in one double bed. He and his brothers hadn't started the saying about two nights, but they had certainly understood what it meant.

In the summer it was so hot the boys couldn't breathe. As soon as they had reached high school age, they'd spent many nights in sleeping bags under the trees, preferring the occasional company of slithering reptiles to the heat in their bedrooms. Their God-fearing Methodist parents didn't have to try very hard to get them to attend church. The boys already knew what hell felt like and didn't want to chance eternal assignment to such quarters.

As the Nebraska wind blew through the upstairs rooms, Adam sat on his bed. Hand-sewn quilts that had been there when he was a child still covered the bed. His drawings of Disney cartoons - he had been sure at one time that he would become a great artist - still hung on the walls. He forced himself to think about his childhood and the old woman with the knife.

If he didn't think about her, if he couldn't confront her in the room in which she had made his life so miserable - he would fail. He would have to drive back home, knowing she (or it), had won. Her prize would be his eternal torment.

Adam vividly remembered being about eight or nine years old when the crazy woman first ran out of the spare room, turned down the hall, and burst into his room. Running straight at him, a look of madness frozen onto her old and wrinkled features, she had worn a Victorian era dress and a reddish-purple hat with a large, synthetic flower on the front. Her face looked to have been garishly made-up, as if she had rubbed handfuls of rouge into her skin. In her right hand she had carried a huge knife.

Just as she was about to deliver the killing blow and cut off his screams forever, she disappeared into thin air. Never tiring for one so old, she didn't attack just once a night, but time, after time, after time. The attacks occurred nightly, without fail, until he'd left for college. He had never spent a night in the house since.

Adam figured she was one of Satan's minions his fundamentalist Sunday schoolteachers warned him about every Sunday. The old woman was to escort his soul to the burning fires of hell after chopping his body into little pieces. Chosen as her victim, he guessed, because he often had lewd and lascivious thoughts while sitting in God's house.

"And that's why I'm back here alone," he said into his cell phone as he sat on the crumbling steps of the house.

Julie, his wife of twenty years, listened on the phone in their home in Boulder. Even before she spoke, he knew her reaction would have been the same if he had told her he was going to run off and join the circus. "I knew I couldn't tell you this at home because of your reaction. You would find some reason for me to forget about doing the most important research in my life."

"Let me get this straight," she said, taking an audible sip of her favorite merlot before continuing. "You haven't decided if a crazy woman who haunted your nights and carried a huge knife, who lived in a closet, a presence only you could see when you were a child, was a ghost of a real person or just your overactive, preadolescent imagination? You have to stay in that dirty old farmhouse and try to discover which it was?

"Adam, I try to understand you since you took your way-too-early retirement. Many people keep working after a heart attack, but not you! I swear you've reverted to your childhood.

"I even tried to understand why you spent all last summer driving around in a stupid little camper, playing in small town golf tournaments, pretending you were some big touring pro. You never even came home with a last place trophy! But this is too much. Tell me you want to go back to discover your roots. Go stay in a motel - if there are any out in the sticks - talk to some of your old friends and relatives, and then get back to civilization. I wouldn't understand, but I could live with that. But don't tell me you're going back to stay in an old house and see if a ghost runs out and tries to hack you into little pieces."

Adam had learned to wait politely for his turn to speak, often withstanding cruel judgments from the woman he had married and felt honor-bound to placate. "I didn't ask you to come along or even to approve of the trip. I know you well enough after all these years to understand you don't care if I'm not there. I didn't expect you to come with me. I don't see why it's such a big deal. You've got your work and have never been dependent on me for how you spend your time."

When she spoke again, her inflection had changed from incredulousness to great pleasure: a cat toying with a mouse. "Of course I don't care. Have a good time. I'll be in Steamboat, where I will make it my personal mission to luxuriate in the mountains while you're in that house. I think I'll stay at the lodge this time instead of a condo. Totally pamper myself. It'll even be more fun when I think about you running around an abandoned house trying to find a ghost in a closet."

"Go ahead, dear. Have your fun," Adam replied. Long ago he had learned the futility of arguing with her. He knew her trip was just to torment him - after all, the Colorado high country was his favorite place on earth. "Who knows? Maybe I'll wrap this up quickly and drive over and join you," he told her. "Maybe we could fool around in the hot tub."

"Now don't you bother about me," she said, the edge in her voice telling him she didn't want him along. "I'll be just fine alone. But I do wonder why you have to be in Nebraska at all. You spent a lot of money on psychiatrists trying to figure out your demons. Remember? Remember what they all agreed on?"

Adam had hoped to get through this without her bringing his mental health up again, but she always did. He was sure it was her way of letting him know she considered him damaged goods and not worthy of her. "Well," he replied sheepishly, as if he were a child trying to explain why his hand was in the cookie jar. "Maybe they were wrong. Maybe they weren't as smart as they thought they were. Shrinks have to tell you that everything has to do with your relationship with your mother. Head doctors always blame our troubles on our mothers. But what if they were wrong? What if they were just grasping at straws because they wanted to get back out on the golf course? Maybe there are ghosts here. Maybe I was the only one who could see them."

"Oh, good comeback, Adam. You're regressing. Let's go over this one more time," she said, speaking with the voice of an erudite professional. "So, you had night terrors as a child, either unable to sleep or waking-up in the middle of the night screaming. Now that's true, isn't it?"

"Sure it is. You know it is. I've told you about it many times."

"And sometimes you still have those same fears, don't you?"

"You should know. You always tell me how I scream after you wake me up. None too gently either." He hoped a display of anger would get her off course.

"Okay." She went on without a trace of compassion in her voice. "Didn't you say you always saw a garishly painted woman wearing a hat with a flower on it and a look of madness in her eyes rushing at you with a huge knife?"

"Of course. That's what I told you. How else would you know?" Increasing anger accompanied his voice. "But what about you? You won't do anything to face your fear of heights. Maybe you should go skydiving. Maybe I'm just braver than you are."

"Adam quit being a butt. I'm just trying to help. Now we both agree, don't we? Your mother had a strange way of disciplining you when you got too rambunctious."

"Yeah. I'll play along, Madam Freud. Yes. I think what she did might even be considered abusive in today's circles."

"And what was that? Please tell me again. Speak plainly and slowly so I know that you understand exactly what you are saying?"

"Okay, here goes. As plainly and as slowly as possible." He remembered his mother's words as clearly as if she had just spoken them. "She always said if I didn't settle down, she was going to get out the butcher knife and turn me into a girl."

"And did you believe her?"

"I don't see how I could have believed that. I loved my mom. Besides, she said it to my brothers, and they didn't have those fears."

"True, true." She replied pensively, as if he had made her stop and consider her faulty psychoanalysis, something he often wished he had done with those overpriced shrinks. "But didn't your last head-healer help you add another piece to the puzzle? One that only affected you, not your brothers?"

"Yes, but . . ."

"No 'yes buts.' What was it?"

"Mom wanted a little girl so much after the birth of my older brother that she dressed me up in dresses and told everyone I was her beautiful little daughter."

"And how long did she do this?"

"All the time Dad was in the service. Until I was about three, I think."

"And do you remember it?"

"I told you, I think I can. Maybe one time on a beach. Besides, she told me and everybody else in the country about it - how I had been such a pretty little girl and how she wished I still was."

She had him. Assault by logic was what she did best. She was turning her version of thumbscrews. "Can you really say those psychiatrists were reaching too far when

17

they said your fears were of your mother coming to castrate you, to turn you back into her pretty little girl? Sounds gruesome to me. A ten-year-old boy thinking his mother was going to lop off his tally whacker and cut off his balls to remake him into a girl. Sometimes, I think she succeeded more than you will ever know."

He had to admit that, in hearing it all again, he couldn't argue with her logic. But he also knew he would never be rid of his demons until he spent time in the house alone. "Whatever," he replied. "It's something I have to do. I know what you're saying is true intellectually, but I need to feel it emotionally. It's the same as you obsessing about your latest research and running off to libraries and laboratories across the country to make sure you're on the right track."

"This isn't about me," she said defensively. "It's about you. I think searching for a ghost in Nebraska is just foolish. But go ahead. Remember, while you're on the flatlands I'll be in Steamboat. Since you're looking for the ghost of a crazy woman, maybe I'll find a still-living stud-muffin to keep me company."

CHAPTER THREE

ADAM REMAINED SITTING ON THE STEPS AFTER TURNING OFF his phone. He stared across the plains, thinking he knew of only two things that never changed. The first was his marriage. The second was the Nebraska prairie. When he gazed beyond the buildings and looked past golden fields of wheat and corn growing in green circles, he could see the land looked as it had for thousands of years.

Sand-drifts along the sidewalk reminded him that living on the plains meant dependency on arid soil. Farmers in areas covered with rich, dark loam who grow bounteous crops year after year love their soil. In western Nebraska people love what the ground produces but find it difficult to care for the dirt.

The huge dust storms of the Great Depression were history only because improved farming methods prevented large tracts of land from blowing away all at once. Even so, finely granulated dirt covered the leaves of corn and dashboards of cars as talcum coats a baby's bottom. Granules of soil had floated in his father's morning coffee and spiced his mother's fried chicken. After being at the farm for fewer than thirty minutes, Adam could already feel it on his teeth. One more day and he would blow it from his nose.

His grandfather had built the house during an age of growth and hope on the table between Medicine Lodge Creek and the North Platte River. In those years, all across the western prairies, farmers plowed up the sod. Immigrants and easterners eager to own land hastily erected new houses, barns, and towns. Sadly, Adam couldn't help but notice the opposite was now true. The children of the original farmers had moved away to more prosperous areas. Many of the deserted farmhouses and barns were run-down. The rest were no longer standing.

Even though he hated the old house, Adam didn't like seeing it begin to resemble the others. He'd thought it would always look as it did in his dreams. But as the jungle does in reverse, he noted, the prairie strives to destroy what man builds. Instead of growing around buildings and covering them with vines, the prairie tears them down, returning man's puny structures to flat, gold, and brown.

Flecks of green, the color Adam's father had last painted the house, clung determinedly to the gray and decaying siding his grandfather had nailed into place more than eighty years ago. Tumbleweeds blocked each of the doors and the brick chimney, caught in a losing battle with gravity, balanced at an ungainly angle. Thankfully, he couldn't see any broken windows and the doors remained closed, the padlocks hanging from them reminiscent of crack-house doors after police raids.

As he walked back into the house, his heart threatened to crash through his chest - exactly the way it had at bedtime when he was ten. Hastily, he dropped his cell phone onto the table next to the suitcase. The surrounding silence magnified the sound it made when it bounced off the table and onto the floor.

He hadn't noticed before how quiet the house was, as if something had banished noise. He felt unwelcome, an intruder in his childhood home where the living were no longer welcome.

"Adam, Goddammit!" he said aloud in an involuntary reaction to the stifling void. "Get a freaking grip. There isn't a crazy woman upstairs and the house is just a bunch of old wood and plaster. There's only life when people are here. It's an inanimate object! Listen to talk radio, play some music, get up and dance. You have to provide the life."

He felt compelled to think out loud. Energized by the sound of his voice and the click of the refrigerator starting as electricity returned, Adam turned on the radio by the sink and enjoyed the twanging guitars and nasal-voiced country music playing on the local station. The drum pounding in his chest slowly returning to normal, he rededicated himself to his purpose. He would give life back to the house and rid himself of terror.

Assured once again that he was grown-up, Adam started looking around. He even ventured upstairs to enter the room where the crazy woman had lived. "Look at that little closet. It's more like a bookcase! Nobody could live in there, and if she does, she has to be more than ninety by now. I could take her in a fight. Besides, what's she been eating in this deserted place? There's no food or water. Nobody's going to run out and chop me up."

Logic - the beauty and poetry of sheer logic spoken by a grown man protecting the child living in his memory. His words, his logic. Of course, there was no crazy woman, and there were no ghosts either. He couldn't feel them. He couldn't sense their presence.

Adam busied himself the rest of the afternoon with opening doors and windows, dusting and sweeping, hooking the propane bottle to the stove, putting his clothes away, and making the bed downstairs in what had been his parent's bedroom. He didn't have time to think about crazy women, big knives, or scary ghosts.

After a light supper of yogurt, salad, and iced tea, he went into the living room and sat in his father's favorite recliner. With a cool breeze washing over him, he finally felt free of his childhood terrors.

As he watched the moonrise over the prairie's horizon, his thoughts drifted to the good times he had enjoyed with his family in that room. It was where they had always put their Christmas tree, where he and his brothers slept on the floor on hot summer nights, and where his father had hooked up their first TV - stringing the wire from the antenna mounted on the roof through the wall, just in time for the World Series. You could see the baseball if you stared hard enough, he recalled with a smile.

"I was just a terrified little boy," he said aloud, keeping his new habit of self-speak. "I loved Mom, and I still think of her as the nicest person in the world, but underneath it all I suppose I really was afraid she was going to cut my pecker off. I was just more sensitive than my brothers." Adam laughed as he remembered their sibling rivalry. It would take a stretch of imagination to call his brothers sensitive.

"Ten o'clock. Time to turn in. I'm sleeping downstairs because it's so much cooler. I am not wimping-out by not sleeping upstairs. I'll spend time looking around upstairs in the morning before it gets too hot."

CHAPTER FOUR

ADAM AWOKE IN TIME TO SEE THE PINK, EARLY MORNING rays of the sun creep over the horizon - something he never did back in the city. The Nebraska wind blowing through the window had been refreshing, and his sleep uninterrupted. He'd had neither nightmares nor visits from knife-wielding ghosts, just hours of peaceful sleep.

While on the farm and in his mother's kitchen, it felt natural to do as she had done. Soon bacon was sizzling in an old cast iron skillet followed by four eggs basting in the grease. Instead of fresh milk - no cows had been on the farm for twenty years - he drank orange juice from the carton.

After washing the dishes, he started up the stairs to examine the rooms that had frightened him as a child, but this time he intended to see them through the eyes of an adult. Steps that haunted his dreams as the passageway to terror didn't look at all as he'd remembered. Instead of steep and dark with flitting shadows and creaking boards warning demons to be ready, they were ordinary stairs to the second floor bedrooms his grandfather had built many decades ago.

The upstairs was a museum of his childhood, including the hole-in-the-wall where Adam had nearly killed his best friend showing him how his older brother's 12-gauge shotgun worked. He had known better than to play with guns, but the shotgun was lying on his model airplane, and his brother shouldn't have left it loaded. He'd always chalked it up to either pure luck or God's will that he hadn't had to live with blood on his hands.

He opened the doors to the built-in closet where, as a ten-year-old, he was sure the crazy woman hid. Instead of a knife-wielding maniac, he found his parent's book collection. Among the volumes were his high school and college annuals, all arranged in chronological order. He made several trips hauling them down to the kitchen and then sat at his mother's yellow Formica kitchen table drinking iced tea, laughing at the pictures, and reading every word written on the inside covers by friends.

Absorbed in the annuals until late in the afternoon, he suddenly realized he hadn't looked around the basement. His search would have been incomplete without poking through the tiny, concrete-walled room where they had waited out so many storms. The basement door opened vertically as though it had once been an opening to an outdoor, underground shelter. He remembered to grab the flashlight from a small shelf. The only light in the small room was a light bulb hanging from the ceiling, and the flashlight was to help locate the cord. If you bumped into it in the dark, the bulb would dance wildly from side to side.

Adam found the light easily, but it began whirling as he fumbled with the switch. Even with shadows dancing across the room, the cellar was no more ominous than any other small room filled with a furnace. A few shelves still held jars of peaches his mother had canned years ago. He also found a box of 20-gauge shotgun shells he had carried pheasant-hunting as a boy, stalking the Nebraskan plains as if he were a hunter on African safari.

Filled with confidence and sympathy for the frightened boy he had once been, Adam ate another light dinner and went to bed downstairs again. The wind blowing across his body was so cool he added blankets. Snuggling into the covers, he thought of how the shrinks had been correct. His fears were merely leftover childhood terrors. He had lived in fear of a house that wasn't haunted. He felt elated - and a little ashamed.

Now that he had found the answer, Adam felt it was the right time to rebuild his relationship with his wife. With more patience and by working harder, he would restore a marriage that once held such promise. He called Julie to tell her the good news - and how much he loved her.

"Oh, it's you," she knew who he was from the caller I.D. on her phone. "How's it going? Ready to call Ghost Busters yet?"

Ignoring the giggle in her voice, Adam enthusiastically told her his news. "Babe, this is just another old house. It's not even a very big one, and it's full of memories, not ghosts or crazy women. It probably sounds silly to you, but I'm really proud of conquering this. I can't wait to be back in the mountains with you. I'm going to leave early in the morning, stop at home, pick up my clubs and fly rod, and join you in Steamboat for dinner. Make reservations someplace luxurious, and get us a tee time for early the next morning."

"Adam, I'm happy you found the answer. I really am. Maybe now you can go back to work. But I've already have reservations, and I was only able to get a room for one. They're having a big festival there and everything is taken. I don't think I can find a room for two, and I hate to lose the one I have."

Usually, anger would have crept into his voice as she rejected him once again, but this time nothing could spoil the occasion. "Okay," he said, still wanting her to be as excited as he was. "Yeah. I'm thrilled. I can't wait to tell you about it. In fact, what I've felt today is peace and belonging. I've never felt that here before. I feel close to my family, as if Mom and Dad are here with me."

"Oh wonderful," she yawned. "Well, I've got an early tee time tomorrow morning on that new course. You know, the one you wanted to play last time but couldn't. I'll tell you what it's like, but I need to get to bed now if I'm going to get up that early."

Ignoring the worms of anger burrowing into his brain, Adam also couldn't wait to get to bed. Another night of uninterrupted sleep would be conclusive. His snores would be the death knell of his fears. He was asleep as soon as he put down the phone, but it was long before morning when he awakened to the wind blowing hard across the room.

He threw off the blankets and started to get up to close the window, almost hitting two eerily glowing figures with his legs as he swung off the bed. A male and female dressed in old-fashioned clothing were holding hands and standing motionless. He stared at them and saw the young woman was crying while the boy wore an expression of rage on his translucent face. Adam reached out to them and, dismayed, watched them disappear. He was alone, standing in front of an open window with his arms outstretched, a strong wind blowing the curtains above his head.

"My God! What was that? Am I awake or asleep? Was that real or a dream?" Adam spoke loudly, hoping to wake up again and return to reality, except he was already awake. "Oh. Sure. I was sleepwalking. That's it. Dreaming and sleepwalking at the same time. That's the obvious part. There are no ghosts."

The silence of the house was overwhelming. Except for the wind, there was no sound. His voice had to fill the void. "That's because nothing electrical is on, you dope. I'll just go out to the kitchen, get an ice-cold can of soda, sit at the table, listen to a little talk radio, and then I'll be ready to go back to sleep."

As he walked through the dining room to the kitchen, the house still seemed too quiet, too empty, and too devoid of life. He hurriedly switched on every light and opened the refrigerator door so its small bulb added to the brightness. As he drank a soda, he listened to agriculture futures on the radio. After a fifteen-minute discussion about sowbellies, he decided it was safe to go back to bed.

Adam crawled under the covers again, believing he had just experienced the most vivid dream of his life. The partially closed window had reduced the wind to a gentle breeze. He felt great. *'Strong winds and a strange diet in a house I used to be afraid of,'* he thought. *'Anybody would have weird dreams.'* Reassured, he fluffed up the pillows and fell asleep again as quickly as he had the first time.

He awakened to a cold wind moaning eerily through the trees of his grandfather's windbreak. Adam was walking over to close the window when he saw her. She looked just as she had when he was a kid, only this time she was screaming. Her voice was shrill above the howling wind.

She ran across the room toward him with the horrible knife raised above her head in the stabbing position. She wore the same off-colored hat. In the moonlight he could see the garish red on her face wasn't make-up, but a glistening liquid smeared across her skin - it looked like blood! Her screams rang in his ears. He stared in panic until she disappeared in the same fashion his earlier visitors had. Even though the apparition had been visible only for a second, sweat poured off his body.

"Jesus!" His voice filled the panic-drained room. "I've heard if you're dreaming and fall over a cliff and hit the ground at the bottom, you'll die, even if you are lying in bed. What would have happened if she'd stabbed me?" Sleep was out of the question for the rest of the night; it would take that long to convince himself the sighting had been just another dream.

"It was just a dream. Had to be. I woke up as soon as it was over. How could she not have appeared?" Adam asked nervously as he grabbed a bottle of Johnny Walker Red and filled one of his mother's old juice glasses to the top. "I've thought about her for years, always associating her with this house. The important thing is how I feel now - how I use this dream to purge her from my subconscious."

The realization the old spook hadn't looked at all as if she were his mother coming to cut off his balls filled him with joy. She was someone he had never seen before, and she appeared addled. He wasn't happy; however, to have noticed the blood covering the spirit's face which, with the screams, constituted two additions to his old dream.

Maybe the booze was working its magic, but he became convinced the appearance had been the old girl's swan song. His rapidly healing psyche had brought her back for an encore performance. She'd attacked with her knife, and he was still alive and cured of his terrors. He wanted the house to know he was a survivor. "That's enough! I'm out of here tomorrow. I'm cured. Those were just dreams, and they weren't even of my mother. In two days I'll be in a float tube catching trout in a mountain lake. I don't need any more of this. I'm going back to bed."

To bed, but not to sleep. As he lay there, she came back - her high-pitched wail bouncing off the bedroom walls. She burst through the wall straight at him, holding the knife in her right hand, blood dripping from her face.

For the first time, he smelled her. She carried the metallic, coppery odor of freshly butchered meat. He could hear her, see her, and smell her. She existed, and he was alert enough to analyze what was happening. "This is no dream," he said, his words filling the cavernous silence. "I don't ever remember odors in a dream. This has to be real."

Adam leaned forward to intercept her rush, raising his arm to grab the hand with the knife, ready to wrestle with a ghost to save his life. As his arm went up in a blocking action, she slammed to a stop faster than he had ever thought humanly possible. She wasn't human; no human was that quick - she was the ghost of his nightmares. As a little boy, an actual ghost had haunted him. The crazy woman had never been a dream.

He sprang to his feet and faced her, less than three feet separating her unearthly form from his strangely calm physical being, but this time she was different. She wasn't wearing that ugly hat. Her hair was dark and long, and she had on a different dress. She looked much younger, and he was sure he'd seen her before. In fact, he had hugged and kissed her when she had been alive and much older. Even with drops of blood streaming across her face, he recognized Sarah Roberts, his grandmother.

He waited for the downward thrust of the terrible blade when she suddenly dropped the knife, placed her now empty hands over her eyes, and cried, "No! No! I didn't! I couldn't! Please! No!"

Then she was gone. No knife was on the floor. Where blood had splattered from her face onto the carpet and bedspread, he could see no stains. He remained where he was standing until a dog barking on a distant farm and the howling reply of a pack of coyotes jerked him from his trance-like state.

Adam was still considering his grandmother's appearance, lying on his back with hands locked behind his head, when sunlight suddenly poured into the room - not the faint hues of early morning - but sun-high-in-the-sky daylight.

"Shit!" he screamed loud enough to be heard in the barn. "I don't remember going back to bed. What happened after Grandma disappeared?" Even talking out loud didn't help. He didn't remember lying down and going to sleep after he saw her. He began doubting her manifestation had been real.

"What if it had all been only another dream? I drank a little Johnny Walker, went back to bed, had a dream, and slept until noon. Hell of a ghost-buster I am."

As he drank coffee at the old kitchen table on a yellow, padded chair with tears in the plastic covering, the truth hit him harder than his older brother had when he had belted him with a baseball bat. This was just as it was when he was a kid. He had been sure he was awake during the second and third visits by the unnatural beings, but now he wasn't so sure.

The logic center of his brain surged into high gear. "That had to be just another dream, you dumb old fart," he yelled. "You dreamed you saw a ghost and jumped out of bed. A peripatetic dream. You didn't even get out of bed. You were still there with the covers pulled up long after the sun was high in the sky. You slept soundly the entire night." He could see that wasn't quite true, however. The half-empty Johnny Walker bottle was still on the cupboard where he had left it.

He had slept, dreamed, drank, and dreamed some more.

CHAPTER FIVE

THE CAFFEINE IN THE COFFEE WAS EXACTLY WHAT ADAM needed. He had a new plan. Even though it meant delaying his trip to the mountains by one day, he had resolved to search the house more thoroughly. If ghosts were inhabitants of a parallel universe, some evidence of their previous earthly existence had to remain. If what he had seen weren't hallucinations or dreams, there had to be a reason they were haunting this house - and him. He was going to use a crowbar and hammer and, if necessary, tear the place apart. He didn't know what he expected to find, but he had to see for himself if anything existed that held spirits in the house.

"Babe," Adam told the voice mail at the hotel where his wife was staying in Steamboat, "Something's come up. I'm going to take one more day to look around. Bye."

His parent's walk-in closet had been the second scariest place in the house when he was a child. Located in the space under the stairs to the second floor and enclosed by walls and a locked door, the inside wasn't even dusty. Adam spent an hour smashing holes in nearly one-hundred-year-old plaster and prying up flooring. When he finished, the closet looked as if a twister hit it, but he had found nothing sinister.

Next, he attacked the upstairs built-in closet where he had found the annuals and had once believed to be the crazy woman's hideout. Again, he found nothing more than wood and the plaster his grandfather had carefully troweled onto the wall. A search of every room in the house followed. As a would-be ghost hunter, he destroyed a ton of plaster and a forest of wood, almost tearing apart the kitchen counters and cupboards, but he failed to find any reason to explain why spirits would want to stick around.

He felt exhausted. The house was a disaster, but he had proven it was empty of life-forms, good or evil. His childhood home held no secrets.

He believed that if something had created a haven for the unnatural, he would have found it. "Think about it." He told himself. "I know everyone whoever lived in this house. I'm directly related to all of them. No crazy woman ever lived here. The only two women ever to occupy the place were Mom and Grandma. I can't believe either of them would purposely haunt me, and both of them were still alive when I started seeing the crazy woman."

Adam was back to square one. He had been afraid of his mother's castration threats after all. There was no point in staying there alone and talking to himself any longer.

He packed his belongings and walked out to his car without locking the front door. He was going to drive to the next largest town, eat the biggest steak he could order in the nicest restaurant he could find, drink the better part of a twelve-pack of beer, and chase it all with Johnny Walker. When he finished drinking, he was going to sleep in a motel and drive straight back to Boulder in the morning.

He would phone his older brother, Jake, tell him about the damage, and never step foot inside the old house again. Jake could lock the door when he came out to survey the damage, and deduct the cost of fixing it up from the rent - if he ever found anyone who wanted to live there.

'Yeah. *And if I had a feather up my ass we'd both be tickled,*' he thought as he hurled his suitcase into the backseat.

Adam wanted one last look around the farm. He decided to walk the grounds, look in the chicken house, climb to the top of the granaries as he had as a kid, and walk the lane their cows had taken to the pasture

Behind the house he saw with sadness what little remained of the lilac bushes and rhubarb. His mother and grandmother had been proud of growing the most fragrant lilacs on the table, and they had so much rhubarb they hadn't been able to give it all away. Adam couldn't stand it, but everybody else in his family had thought rhubarb pie to be the most delicious dessert ever invented.

Strange, he thought, looking over the detritus that remained from years of neglect. Branches as big as logs were scattered among a few spots of wilted, brown rhubarb but no lilacs grew there. He supposed people from all over the community came and dug the plants to start their own plots. Adam thought that was great - the blossoms his relatives had prized lived on, gracing farms and homes around the community.

Reaching down to pick a piece of the emaciated rhubarb, tempted to taste it, he noticed the plot was a depressed space, although he remembered it as raised. That also made sense. The people who took the plants would have taken some topsoil with them. What he couldn't figure out, however, was why the depression seemed almost exactly square. It appeared to be the outline of an old foundation.

Coyotes, foxes, and wandering farm dogs had discovered the plentiful supply of rabbits living around the house and had been digging-up burrows in the soft earth where the lilacs had grown. He walked over to gaze at a hole where the fox had literally caught the hare. Fur and smatterings of blood marked the dirt. It was easy to see why the animals had torn the area apart, the holes were not deep, and in places the sun reflected off bare metal.

Curious to find what it was, he grabbed a shovel from the front porch and began scooping dirt off steel that was strong enough to neither bend nor break. The sound of the shovel hitting the metal was not what he expected. Striking a piece of buried machinery should have produced a muted, solid noise without vibration or ringing. This was different. The tones had a muffled sound, but they were definitely bell-like.

Adam threw dirt in every direction until heavy sheets of welded steel plating became visible. After two hours of shoveling, he stepped-off the dimensions of the metal, measuring it at twelve by twelve. He couldn't remember anybody ever talking about buried steel under the lilacs, and he would have remembered something such as that.

Adam's grandfather had always said that on a day so hot the chickens laid hard-boiled eggs. Working as quickly as possible under a Nebraska sun that was growing hotter with each minute, he began to suspect the old man had been right. He cleared an edge of the metal sheet that was more than one half-inch thick. As he uncovered more of the plating, he realized it sat on a foundation of limestone rocks indigenous to the prairie.

After clearing the debris from along the wall, Adam found an opening where a door had once been. He quickly pulled away the rocks and dirt. Lying flat on his stomach, he stuck his head into the opening. A stench of dirt, decay, and something a longtime dead hit him. Because the afternoon sun was disappearing in the opposite direction, no light entered the opening.

He jumped to his feet, glad to be away from the odor, and sniffed the clean prairie air one more time. After filling his lungs with fresh air, he knelt down and crawled as far under the steel as he could while holding his breath, and shined a flashlight around the small room.

"*Oh shit!*" he screamed loud enough to scare a flock of pheasants using the old trees as roosts. Gasping in horror, no longer noticing the horrible stench, he stared into the eyeless sockets and grinning mouth of a human skeleton. Recovering his senses and shining the light around the small tomb, he swore again when the light illuminated a second set of remains.

CHAPTER SIX

RUSTING, TIME-STIFFENED HINGES HELD THE KITCHEN DOOR to the wall. They were more difficult to remove than he had thought they would be. When the door was finally free of the frame, he carefully slid it under the remains, determined to transport them into the house intact. Intuitively, he knew the fears ruling his life had a connection to the bodies. Freeing them from the disgrace of an unmarked steel-topped tomb would also set him free. By honoring them with a proper burial, he would escape his psychological imprisonment.

Most of the clothing, except for a few scraps so decayed neither color nor texture remained, had disappeared. Exquisite silver rings still circled the finger bones of one of the skeletons, and a turquoise and silver comb, the kind Spanish women wore in the old Southwest, lie by the top of the skull. Near the other skeleton, he found a small silver belt buckle with strands of old leather clinging to it. A stiletto with a five-inch blade, the handle ornate with silver and turquoise, lie near the pelvic bones.

After recovering his composure, Adam ate a snack of bananas and apples, the only food in the house he didn't think would taste like decayed bodies. He washed the fruit down with liberal amounts of Johnny Walker and called his wife to tell her, in the gentlest terms possible, what he'd uncovered. Declining her demand that he call the police and return to Colorado immediately, he began planning how to find out who the skeletons had been and what they could possibly have done to deserve such a grisly fate.

———

The sun was already heating the dusty streets of the small town of Medicine Lodge early the next morning when he entered the Old Settlers Museum housed in the antiquated Union Pacific depot the railroad had abandoned in 1948. Several years earlier, the Medicine Lodge Historical Association had taken the depot over, fixed it up, and used it to showcase local history. It was a small one-room building with seats around the edges and a ticket counter in the center, which now served as the curator's desk. The wooden building contained a myriad of artifacts, antiques, and pictures of pioneers. Some sat on pedestals, pins held others to the walls, and a glass case displayed a copy of a yellowed newspaper, *The Medicine Lodge Plains Voice*, dated 1919.

Adam had just entered the room, eyes adjusting to the muted light, millions of dust particles visible under skylights in the high ceiling, when a woman's voice called out a greeting.

"Good Morning. My goodness, you startled me. We aren't used to visitors so early in the morning. I'll be with you in a jiffy."

He turned towards the sound, but all he could see of the speaker was the back of her head as she worked behind a diorama showing how Plains Indians, before their acquisition of horses, drove buffalo over a cliff above the creek. "Uh. Fine. Take your time," he answered, wondering if she was someone he knew. "I'm just looking around. When you have time, I'd like to ask you a few questions."

The museum was clearly a testimony to the strong, God-fearing pioneer farmers who had turned sod, built fences, and grew crops. He saw a few displays about Native Americans, mainly the buffalo cliffs, and almost nothing about the cattle-ranchers who had been the first Anglo-Americans to settle on the land.

Rows of early plows, pictures of farmers standing beside steam engine tractors and thrashing machines, and a corner devoted to dresses worn by sturdy pioneer women and their babies dominated one side of the room. Across from the clothing was a display of Bibles with local family names imprinted on plastic tape identifying each one. Adam knew most of the names and spent several minutes reading lists of births and deaths, both including quite a few of his friends. He had never seen his family's Bible. He didn't even know if they had one.

"What can I help you with? Just passing through or do you know anybody from around here? We don't get many strangers."

Adam looked up and saw the woman standing beside the display she had been working on, smiling, her voice friendly and genuine. Her nametag read Cynthia Schmidt, which wasn't a great surprise since more Schmidts lived around Medicine Lodge than photos of Smiths and Joneses graced post office walls.

"Well, well," she said, sounding shocked but pleased. "Look what the cat drug in. After your folks passed away so suddenly, I never thought we'd see you around these parts again."

Tall, five feet eight inches or so, thin but nicely filling out a sundress, she looked more like someone he expected to meet on the Boulder Mall than in a dusty small town museum. Adam guessed she was over forty but pleasantly preserved - and he hated it when someone knew him and he didn't know them. "I'm sorry, but who are you?" he asked, feeling stupid.

Her quick smile mitigated his feelings of awkwardness. "I didn't expect you would remember me." Walking towards him, her voice catching a little and her hips moving in a delightfully feminine fashion, she led with both arms out straight, and he realized she was about to hug him. He searched her face for clues and barely had time to blurt out, "Larson twins," before her arms enveloped him.

She pulled away, gave him a soft kiss on the corner of his mouth, and stared into his eyes from a very close distance "Not the twins. I'm their younger sister. Remember, I was a freshman in high school when you guys were seniors. I know this is silly to tell you, but I don't think I've ever gotten over the crush I had on you, and me, a married woman with grandchildren." Then, with a flirtatious and alluring look, she asked, "Should I be ashamed of myself?"

Emotions and hormones Adam had forgotten about swirled around inside his body like the violent winds of a plains tornado. He remembered her as a pretty little stick of a freshman who always had been near her sisters whenever he'd tried to ask one of them out. "Sure. I remember you. You were always in the way when I was hitting on your sisters. You blocked my best moves."

"Now you know why," she laughed, keeping her arms around him and staring directly into his eyes. "I made Kari and Shari promise never to go out with you. They had to save you for me. You never asked me out, but you never had a date with one of them either."

A bell attached to the door tinkled gently as it opened. Cynthia's ears picked up on the soft sound. She pulled away and started shaking his hand as a burley teenager wearing a Nebraska football jersey burst in and yelled in a croaking voice, "Grandma, Let's go. You know you've got to take me to baseball practice. Hurry up or I'll be late."

"Just keep your shirt on, young man," she yelled back while continuing to stare at Adam. "You stay right here," she whispered. "Don't you go anywhere. I'll only be fifteen minutes. We've got almost forty years of catching up to do."

He struggled to reduce his blood pressure and slow his heartbeat. There was no chance he was going to leave. She would be an invaluable aide in his search for clues, and besides, nothing so salacious had happened within thirty feet of him in years.

During the time she was gone, he browsed through all the tiny museum's exhibits. Only two items concerned his family. The first was a picture of his grandfather dressed in cowboy finery. Since Adam had always known him as a farmer, this was a surprise. The inscription under the photo was even more astonishing: "*Cowboy George Roberts wearing his best outfit, including pistol and rifle, 1905.*"

The second photo was of a worn-out wagon carrying two women, a man, a teenage boy, and two small children - one of the women sitting next to the teenage driver holding a lever action rifle. The label read, "*The arrival of Cowboy George's family, 1914.*"

This was all news to him. The hardworking clod-kicker he knew as his grandfather had been enough of a cowboy to have such a nickname, and he'd gotten to town a lot earlier than the rest of his family.

He and his brothers had never heard any stories about their great-grand parents on their father's side. They didn't know where they came from or anything about them. Even more confusing had always been why they had never known their uncles, aunts, or cousins who lived in the same town with a population of fewer than eight hundred. They had known everyone else; they just had never met their own relatives. As far as Adam could remember, he had never spoken to any of them except for a muffled greeting as they passed on the street. He had never been inside their houses, and they had never been in his.

His cousins had driven twenty miles to a bigger town to attend high school. The only time Adam ran into them when they were in high school, his older brother, Jake, and he had soon been in the fistfight of their lives. Their relatives had attacked without warning or provocation. The fight had ended in a draw, and Adam had never seen them again.

Whenever he asked his parents about the split in the family, the answer had always been the same, "We don't know, and if your grandfather does, he refuses to talk about it."

"Hi! Miss me?" Cynthia asked, rushing back through the door. "That was Joey, my youngest grandson. He's the jock in the family. I brought some coffee and doughnuts. You sit right there," she said, pointing at two wooden chairs that could only have been school surplus furniture, "and tell me all about yourself."

He did, and since it had been so long that anyone had shown interest, he related his life's story. He told her how, as a boy, his two loves had been the history of the Old West and the mountains. Even before he'd been a high school freshman, he had already been sick of that, "hot, dry, miserable, damned old dirt farm." He had been to Yellowstone National Park once and knew that was where he should live. He had never felt more at home in his life, spending everyday in the mountains soaking up the cool temperatures, the green freshness, and the smell of pine in the air.

He told her he had known since that magical summer he would never be able to live in Nebraska as an adult. When he finished, she knew he'd left for Colorado to attend college, and had taken ten years off to work as a professional ski patroller and mountaineering instructor before working on a doctorate in history at the University. He ended with how he'd been a junior college American History teacher until taking early retirement after a mild heart attack; that he was married and the father of three grown children; played too much golf; spent too little time fishing; and planned his winters around powder snow, working occasionally as a ski instructor.

She seemed fascinated, frequently interrupting his monologue with sighs, smiles, and comments such as, "Oh. How exciting!" She made him feel more important and successful than he'd felt in years.

"Okay, your turn," he told her, drinking his now cooled coffee. Her reaction to his story had been so endearing, he hadn't even stopped to take a drink or eat a doughnut. As soon as she started, he could see why she thought his life had been so exciting. Married right out of high school, she immediately had three children and was now a grandmother six times over. Outside the museum job, her first, the bright moments in her life were attending University of Nebraska football games.

Her husband owned a small farm and devoted his life to fishing, hunting, and poker - events in which she and the other women in their circle never took part, except to clean-up discarded beer cans and cigarette butts. He guessed that's why his wife's career as a research scientist seemed so exciting to her.

"Boring, I know, to somebody with all your adventures. Goodness! A ski instructor in Colorado!" Cynthia ended her story with enthusiasm about his life and a question, her hand caressing his forearm. "But what brought you back to these parts? You must find this place dull."

"Well, uh, Cynthia," he stammered, trying to keep from staring lustfully. "I just came back to, you know, rediscover my roots. Stay out on the farm. Talk to people. Work on memories. Find out how I got to be me."

"And did your wife, the scientist, come with you? Is she back on the farm making you lunch?"

When he told her his wife was vacationing in Steamboat, Cynthia's smile brightened and she scooted a little closer.

"But, well, it's the strangest deal," he continued, feeling as if he were under the influence of truth serum. "Yesterday, as I was looking around outside the house, I found a hidden grave with two skeletons . . ."

"Oh my God! How terrible for you!"

"Yes. It was horrible." he said in a low voice. "That's why I'm here. I have to find out who they were. They looked to be full-grown. I need to see everything you have about my family. Read old newspapers, research everything about them."

"Adam, everything this museum owns is on display. The old papers are in Lincoln. We're supposed to get copies on film in a year. The state is even putting all local papers on computer, but they won't finish for a couple of more years.

"Let's see," she continued, tapping her lips with her finger. "Have we anything here that would help? I know we have a couple of pictures of your family."

When he told her about his surprise at the picture of his grandfather in cowboy garb and how he didn't know he had arrived in the area before the rest of his family, Cynthia suddenly got up and hurried over to her desk.

"Wait. Wait. There is another one. The pastor just brought it over last week. Said it was the only item in an old file marked *Roberts*." She handed him a picture of two beautiful young women. He immediately recognized one as his grandmother about the same age as he had seen her the night before last, but his eyes jumped to the other - a woman who looked to be several years younger than his grandmother did. She had an ornate silver comb carefully placed into her jet-black hair.

CHAPTER SEVEN

"THIS IS IT! THIS IS THE PLACE! I CAN SEE FOREVER. THE grass is high enough to tickle a horse's belly," Cowboy George Roberts yelled. By sunset the next day he would have the deed to his own place registered in Ogallala. As soon as he dug a well and had enough water for livestock, he'd have a ranch. He couldn't remember being so excited.

All he had ever wanted to be was a cowboy with a ranch of his own. "Don't I know the work good enough?" he hollered at the top of his voice, racing his horse through the grass just starting to turn straw-colored in the summer heat. "Damn, I know it better than most of the pig farmers who call themselves ranchers around here."

Cowboy George was the oldest child of a family of horse and cattle thieves that plagued the range from Texas to Canada. As far back as he could remember, his uncles, aunts, cousins, parents, grandparents, and shirttail relation had labored in the occupation until, one by one, they became guests of honor at local necktie parties. "Shucks," he'd told the other ranch hands at dinner several days earlier, "most of my kin weren't given the dignity of an unfair trial. They were just took to the nearest tree and lynched."

George was only seventeen. Three years earlier he had snuck out of the cave down on the Washita where what remained of his family was hiding out, stole the best horse in the outfit, and struck out on his own. Only fourteen, he had already known he didn't want the life of a horse thief. Since then, he had been drifting, working as a cowboy, and dreaming of having his own place.

He was sorry his good fortune had come at such a price for the rancher he worked for and admired. Old Punk Queen owned most of the land between the North Platte River and the Medicine Lodge Creek where he and his three sons raised beef for the eastern markets. Several weeks earlier, George had found Queen's youngest son, Gurley, sprawled out on his belly in a draw, blood seeping from a jagged tear in his abdomen and chest.

Apparently Gurley had chased one of the longhorns into the gulch and had dismounted to look for the cow when the scrub cedar became too tight to navigate on horseback. George guessed the cow was too close when the kid climbed down. She shook her head and two feet of pointed horn opened him up from neck to pecker.

George had bandaged the kid up the best he could, fashioned an Indian travois out of a couple of cedar logs, and took Gurley home to the big house in Bull Horn Canyon. Even while dragging the dying boy into the yard, George thought the ranch was the most beautiful place he had ever seen. Its high canyons, tall trees, geese honking warnings at his approach, and deer racing away through the thickets made the place seem like paradise. Even on such a sorrowful occasion, all he could think about was having his own place someday.

The other ranch hands knew something bad had happened the minute they saw George pulling a travois behind his horse. The foreman ran to get Punk while another cowboy fetched the old wrangler who knew the most about medicine - the story was the elderly cowpoke had been a sawbones during the Civil War driven to a life of alcohol and hermitage by the horrors he had seen. Three other cowhands carried the moaning boy into the stone house and placed him gently on the oak table imported all the way from England.

Used to the hardships of life on the plains, the ranch hands could tell right away a doctor wasn't necessary. No one could survive in the kid's condition. He was losing too much blood, and his insides were visible through the gash in his belly. After lying on the table for only a short time and calling weakly for his mother, never knowing she was cradling him in her arms, Gurley coughed, spewing a torrent of blood across the new carpet hauled in from St. Louis, opened his eyes, shouted "No!" and died.

For many years, the story told around bunkhouse stoves across western Nebraska was that young Gurley had seen the angels coming to get him. He had yelled out because he didn't want to go, but those ghostly vaqueros hadn't cut him any slack. Gurley became an angel and Punk Queen, knowing Cowboy George's dream of being a rancher, asked him into the house the day of the funeral.

Tears sliding down his cheeks, the young cowhand walked into the parlor where a small wreath fashioned from the dead boy's hair sat on an easel. He wondered how it would have had been to have parents who cared so much. "George," his boss said softly, "Mother and I know how much you want your own place. Would you consider taking part of our range as a living memorial to our son?"

His heart racing, afraid that he had misunderstood, the best George could do was stammer a question. "But, but, Punk, what's a living memorial, he's gonna stay dead, ain't he?"

"Yes, George. Our son will always be dead," Punk's wife answered. "But if you start a successful ranch on part of the land we were going to give him, his memory will live through you."

George had wanted to run over and hug the rancher and his wife, but all he could do was shuffle his feet, "Yes, Ma'am, I reckon I will take some of that land. I'll make it a right nice place you can visit anytime. I promise I won't have any whores there, and I'll always piss somewheres away from the house in case you want to come visiting."

George chose a portion of range devoid of trees or water, but the grass was thick and tall, and he could dig a well next to an old buffalo wallow. He could make enough money to buy cows by selling the buffalo bones that littered his property. There was a big market for bones back east where factories ground them into fertilizer. There were so many on his plot of land that George couldn't take a step without stumbling over a danged skeleton.

Cowboy George picked bones, loaded them onto his wagon, and hauled them to the train depot forty miles away in Ogallala. He hauled them until his back was sore, his wagon broken, and his horse lame. He hauled them in the cold, in the dark, and under the burning sun. He picked bones until his land was clear of them, and he had made enough to buy ten heifers and rent a bull to mount them.

One day, in 1908, George was hanging around the train depot in the new town of Medicine Lodge when a young woman from California who came in on the Union-Pacific to work as a tutor on the Medicine Lodge Cattle Company stole his heart. George spent the better part of a year pursuing his love and finally convinced her to marry him - after he promised to build her a wood frame house.

Over the years that followed, as he and his bride made a little money, enlarged their herd, and he became a respected member of the Cattlemen's Association, Cowboy George still found time to lie on the banks of the wallow and watch the clouds riding free on the wind as he had when he was young.

Later, when Punk Queen's widow put the land surrounding his little ranch up for sale and sold it off in small parcels to farmers who erected barbed wire fences and plowed under the native sod, George kept on raising cattle. The pioneer farmers pointed him out to their families as a throwback to the old days.

CHAPTER EIGHT

ADAM HAD SEEN THE YOUNG WOMAN IN THE PICTURE before. She had been holding hands with a boy who looked just like her when they had appeared before him in his parent's bedroom. The silver comb she had been wearing was now resting beside a skull in an upstairs bedroom of the old farmhouse. Seeing her in a timeworn black and white photograph was too much. He had barely been able to tell Cynthia where he was going as he lurched out to his car.

———

The next morning Adam was in Lincoln, four hundred miles to the east, waiting for the Nebraska Museum of History to open. The information librarian who unlocked the front door extended a warm greeting to the disheveled man banging on the window. Because of her help, he was soon sitting beside a stack of microfilm boxes, reading copies of the *Medicine Lodge Plains Voice*.

Most of the elegantly written pages contained obituaries, births, new arrivals, and stories telling which families visited other farms, ranches, or homes for dinner. Articles told where fences were going up and where gargantuan steam tractors pulling heavy plows had torn up the sod. There were a host of articles about grasshoppers, tornadoes, blizzards, torrential floods, and wilting droughts. However, an article on the first page of the June 4, 1905, issue stunned him. His grandfather had been some kind of hero in the old days.

Tragic Passing of Son of the Open Range

We were saddened to hear of the tragic passing of one of the sons of a North Table rancher. Gurley Queen, a mere sixteen years old and in the flower of his youth, was killed Thursday by a longhorn.

Evidentially, the boy dismounted in heavy brush, only to be impaled on a deadly horn. The poor soul was rescued from the evil beast by Cowboy George Roberts, a drifter and ranch hand employed by the Bull Horn Creek Cattle Company for the past year. Even though the young hero, the same age as the beloved victim, tried his best to administer life-saving help, Gurley died in his mother's arms.

The cowboy who brought poor Gurley home to his mother's bosom will soon become a respected member of the local ranching community. In gratitude for his Herculean efforts in bringing Gurley home alive so that his mother could hold him one last time and comfort him on his way to eternal rest, the grateful parents deeded young Mr. Roberts a small section of their vast holdings. Now the heroic drifter has a ranch of his own. We expect to hear much about him in the future.

How could he have not known this? His grandfather was Cowboy George, a drifter and cowhand awarded the land for the family farm because he bought a dying boy home to his mother? There had to be a mistake, but the land was the dry-land wheat farm in western Nebraska where his family had lived. An article dated three weeks later described the property and even mentioned the buffalo wallow where he and his brothers had played cowboys and Indians.

He saw other family stories typical of small town newspapers: his grandparents wedding announcement in 1909, his father's birth announcement in 1913, frequent mentions of whom they had dinner with, and how his grandfather had been a member of the Masonic Lodge and president of the local cattlemen's association. One article, however, had an ominous but vague reference to the Ku Klux Klan holding a rally at the farm in 1920.

Klan Rallies on North Table

The newly formed North Table Chapter of the Ku Klux Klan rallied on the ranch of George Roberts last Friday afternoon. Events were broken up by gunfire and a fierce storm before a gigantic cross could be torched by the white-robed crowd.

We are happy that no one was injured in the incident, except for a scalded horse. We hope everyone will now come to their senses, resolve their problems by peaceful means, and work together for the benefit of the community.

Adam felt as if his breath had been knocked out, and he couldn't draw another. He knew about the Klan in the Midwest in the early part of the twentieth century. He had even asked his grandfather if had had ever joined the order; his answer had been typical him. "Oh, I went to a meeting when they first got here. They had the best whiskey in the county. Didn't put much stock in what they were saying, but we sure drank a bunch."

If that were true, why did the invisible empire hold a rally at his ranch? Or had it then been a farm? Adam couldn't believe his grandfather had lied to him. He had never known him to be a man of strong prejudice. What about the gunshots and settling matters peacefully?

Brain whirling, struggling with his thoughts, Adam quickly summarized what he knew about the Klan. The former Confederate General Bedford Forest had served as the organization's first president. Its purpose was to control blacks and preserve the white way of life after the Civil War. Defunct at the turn of the century, it regenerated with the 1915 movie, *The Birth of a Nation.* Midwestern Americans had flocked to the Order to protect their way of life from an onslaught of immigrants, minorities, and Roman Catholics, who, according to the Klan, took their orders directly from the Pope.

They were a moralistic group, denouncing the evils of dope, bootlegging, cattle rustling, prostitution, sex, adultery and all other vices including gambling. He'd never been able to reconcile his grandfather's description of their whisky with what they had preached, except to consider that they were as hypocritical as they had been prejudiced.

Other than his grandfather's comments, he couldn't remember hearing anything about the invisible empire in western Nebraska. He knew the Klan had hanged, shot, and burned a black man in Omaha for supposedly assaulting a white woman, and that the group had been extremely powerful in Colorado, even managing to get one of their own elected Governor. The Klan had reached its zenith in membership during the early twenties, a time known as its Second Era.

Leaning back in the chair, mulling everything over, Adam felt a light touch on his shoulder and thought the librarian was issuing him a reprimand for the way he was sitting. As usual, only two chair legs touched the floor.

"You didn't think I was going to let you do all of this hard research alone, did you?" Cynthia Schmidt whispered as she stood over him. When he looked up, her mouth was a lot closer to his than anybody's, other than his wife's, had been in many years.

Seeing her was a surprise but not a shock. Cynthia had mentioned a need to go to Lincoln to check on the filming of the old newspapers, and she had seemed genuinely interested in his search. In fact, she had seemed a lot more interested in his work than that of the Medicine Lodge Museum. "What can I do to help? What do you want me to look for?" she asked.

He told her the gist of his discoveries - about how his grandfather had come to own their land, and about the 1920 Klan rally. Like most Nebraskans, she had never known the guys in white outfits once operated openly in her state. "So look for anything about the Roberts family or the Klan. See if I missed anything," he said, glad to have company and another set of eyes.

She quickly read the issues of the paper and found only the same articles, then she had another idea. "You know the Sidney paper, it was *The Pioneer Bugle* in those days, and it carried news about all the small towns in the county. We should check it also."

Fortunately, the *Pioneer Bugle* was on a CD. Cynthia showed him how to do a query using *Roberts* and *Klan* as keywords. An article in a 1913 issue, written two weeks before the birth of his father, provided a clue about the possible identity of the skeletons.

North Table Rancher Greets Wife's Friends
George Roberts, quickly becoming a well-known rancher, greeted Jesus and Consuelo Vargas as they arrived on the Union-Pacific today. The two brightly dressed young Californians of Mexican descent are here to help care for the rancher's new baby. Brother and sister, they were born in Mexico and grew up on the same ranch as Mrs. Roberts in Orange County, near the present city of Los Angles. They should quickly become invaluable in the busy household.

The only other article found by the search told a great deal more about the rally and what his grandfather hadn't told him about the Ku Klux Klan. It was dated 1920.

Klan Calls On Rancher to Oust Papists
Garl Schwartz, local leader of the North Table Klan, convened the members for a discussion about the foreigners, papists, and adulterers living in their midst. After a great deal of shouting and roars of approval from the gathering, a decision was made to rally at George Roberts's place and convince him to send the Mexican Papist fornicators he has living with him back to wherever they came from.

"My Lord," Cynthia whispered as he read the article over her shoulder. "Do you think that's who the skeletons are? Did the Ku Klux Klan kill them that night and nobody reported it to the police?"

Her eyes widened as she read the piece. "You recognized the comb in the woman's hair, didn't you? You said you saw some artifacts, personal items lying around."

Taking the picture of his grandmother and the other woman out of the manila envelope she carried with her, she went on. "This one. This comb. You found it, didn't you? That's why you got so nervous and left after you saw the picture."

"Yes. I think that's who they were. I found a silver comb just like that one lying by one of the skulls. I also found rings like those around the finger bones."

"I knew it. I knew you saw something in this picture that upset you. That's understandable. What a shock." After giving Adam a hug to bolster his strength, Cynthia spent hours searching the library for anything else about the incident. Just fifteen minutes before closing time - they hadn't stopped for lunch or dinner - she put her hand back on his arm. "There's nothing else for us to find here. I'm starving. Let's go get something to eat and talk about what we're going to do next."

As they were leaving the building, Cynthia pointed to a small blue car and announced she was driving. "I know Lincoln better than you do, and there is this little place down by the stadium that has the best food in town. It's called the Training Table. The owner is a former Husker from a big ranch in the Sand Hills who never made it in the pros. He opened this place to help sell his family beef. It's wonderful!"

The restaurant was that. With a motif of University of Nebraska football, the Training Table served cholesterol-laden meals dominated by huge slabs of beef that would have thrown the trendy, health-conscious people of Boulder into apoplectic seizures. They had no sooner ordered, Cynthia starting with a glass of wine and Adam with a light beer, when she placed her hand on his forearm again, looked straight into his eyes and told him her intentions. "Adam, I want you to come back to my motel and stay with me tonight. I want you to be my Great Affair, to put some excitement into my life. Please say you will!"

He had fantasized she felt that way every since she'd confessed her high school crush had carried over to the present. He hadn't argued when she suggested dinner together, and her showing up in Lincoln hadn't shocked him.

Cynthia had called up his fantasies and offered to make them reality, but he couldn't. Not now! He wanted to stay married. He admired his wife's professionalism and was trying hard to bring the romance back into their relationship. "Oh, uh, aw, I uh. I don't think that . . ."

"Please don't say no, Adam," she interrupted while massaging his arm. "Nobody will ever know. You can trust me. I'm a respectably married grandma. I just want to have one fling in my life, and it's got to be with you.

"I didn't tell you all my life's story when you asked yesterday. I should have, but some of it was too embarrassing. Now I feel as if I've known you for more than one hundred years. Don't say anything until I tell you about me.

"My husband works hard and plays hard. He's either trying to increase the harvest, cut costs by working harder, or hunting and fishing with his buddies. He's just never been emotionally available to the children or me. Sometimes, we go to community gatherings in the park - you remember what they are like. The women all cook fried chicken or baked beans or a desert. Anyway, he could never pick out which children were his when a whole group of them were playing.

"He has no idea what I think, want, or like. When he wants my opinion, as the old joke goes, he gives it to me.

"Don't get me wrong, Art is a good man, a good provider. He never misses a game when his sons or grandsons are playing, and he's never hit me or anything like that. Some days, however, I just want to die, or run away. I'm so lonely for someone to want me, to ask me what I think, to make me feel important - to like me.

"There, I guess I got it out." Cynthia said, smiling and crying at the same time, tears falling onto the tablecloth as she spoke. "I'm just a sad, lonely, old woman looking for someone to be nice to her. Please be that person. If you won't, I don't know what I'm going to do. I'm just not going to trip the milkman and beat him to the floor, although I've thought about it."

Adam looked across the table in the dimly lit restaurant at the still-beautiful woman with tears in her eyes. He didn't have it in him to say no. He couldn't hurt her feelings - even if it hurt him when the affair was over. Besides, he knew all too well what she was talking about. Living with a person who is too busy for you is a lonely existence. He lived there too.

Cynthia drove Adam to her hotel. In anticipation, she had booked a room in the Platte River Hotel in downtown Lincoln. She'd never stayed there before. With a reputation as the finest hotel in Nebraska, it was usually too costly for her limited budget.

"Adam," she said, clutching his arm as they walked through the brass framed, lighted glass doors lining the entrance to the hotel, "I'm going to make this the best night of your life. Just being here with you, after having this same damn crush for forty years - it's bound to be the best night of mine."

She smiled brightly when he placed his hand on hers and said, "I can't think of anywhere I'd rather be right now. Why don't we have a drink? You're beautiful in this light. I want to look at you for a while."

"There's a piano bar on the mezzanine," she said, blushing at the compliment. "The piano player has such a reputation. I've even heard of him out in the sticks. Let's go there."

Seated at a table in the corner, the light dim except for the lamp on the piano lighting the music, Cynthia glanced at Adam, hoping he wouldn't notice her growing embarrassment. Brazen behavior was out of character for her, and even though she had planned this, thoughts of her husband and children swirled through her mind. She was close to telling him she was sorry and running away as fast as she could when the man at the piano began playing her favorite song.

"What is that piece?" Adam asked, breaking the silence. "You know, I saw the movie, I think I was still living in Nebraska. It had that pretty blond actress in it, the one who was so popular back then. All of us boys were in love with her."

"It's my favorite," she whispered softly. "Her name was Sandra Dee and the music is *Theme from a Summer Place*. I have a copy and watch it all the time, mainly just to hear that song."

He smiled over at her, taking his glass of wine the server had brought as she was telling him the name of the movie, lifted it in a toast, and said, "Well. I guess it will be our song. Thank you for bringing me here."

Her embarrassment disappeared. Cynthia was happier than she had been in years. After thirty minutes of laughter, reminiscing about people they both knew, and getting to know each other all again, they were in her room. They made love slowly, not in the heat and breathtaking passion of youth, but with the familiarity of two old friends. Softly. Tenderly. Caringly. Each more concerned about the other.

CHAPTER NINE

AN ALARM TRIGGERED A DEVICE AND ROLLED UP ADAM'S eyelids as if they were spring-driven shades on a farmhouse window. He was awake at three in the morning. He had set an internal alarm the minute he had fallen into Cynthia's arms. This was her Great Affair, her escape from life on the unchanging prairie and an existence painted in the monotonous hues of the brown and gold plains. But she wasn't his great passion. He didn't want to run away from his life. Guilt powered the alarm that interrupted his sleep.

Wine and a beautiful woman had conspired to lessen his inhibitions, filling him with the forgotten characteristics of a young male ego: invisibility and invincibility. Making love had lured them to sleep, the feel of each other's arms and bodies comforting and soothing. As soon as he was awake, however, the feelings of guilt became too intense to ignore. Electrical currents of anxiety raced through his organs and surged down his legs and arms. His fingers and toes tingled as if they were attached to low voltage batteries.

Even though she had been the one who asked, he had wanted to make love to her since he'd first seen her. Not only had he known it was going to happen, he had been as responsible for their sleeping together as she had been.

Cynthia might have spoken the words, but psychologically he had scripted the drama.

Nude, she lay facing him with an expression of contentment. While neither of them looked as good in the morning as they had the night before, she was beautiful in the soft light. He couldn't tear his eyes away from her, and lust began its timeless battle with guilt once again.

He had been afraid she would awaken and find guilt pouring off his skin as sweat did from a farmer on a hot day. Now, she would open her eyes and see how enamored he was. He had to leave. He had to get away so he could control the emotional battle welling up within him. One moment he wanted family and hearth to prevail, the next he was pulling for lust to triumph. Adam would never be able to make up his mind as long as she slept naked next to him.

He loved his wife. Of course he did. Their problems were normal among professional couples, and he didn't want to hurt their tenuous relationship. But Cynthia had promised, and he believed her, that this was her Great Affair, and he had nothing to fear from her. She had assured him no one would ever know about them, and that she would never do anything to hurt his family. When Adam decided it was over, she had promised, it would end without argument or recrimination. They would be friends who had once had privileges, as she called it, but nothing more.

Besides, she had asked, what were two people over fifty going to do, run off and find a judge to marry them when she got pregnant? Would one of them realize he or she couldn't live without the other and force everyone in both families to appear on a reality television program? "The glorious truth about our age," she'd said just before falling asleep, "is that such high drama doesn't happen.

Common sense is what makes being our age livable. We can still act young, but we don't have to be juvenile."

"I know you need to get back and start searching for information about that Klan rally," she murmured, her soft voice breaking the silence. "If it were me, I would be driving back already. Give me a hug and get out of here. I'll be along later."

"No. I'll stay for a while. What kind of guy do you think I am? One who screws and runs?"

"No! You go," she said. "You need time to think. You need time to decide what you feel, and you do need to find out what happened to your grandparent's family. If you're fine with continuing my Great Affair, come see me in the museum. If not, I'm sorry, but I want you to remember that you have been my one affair, and that my life is better because you came back to town. Now go."

Rain was falling softly as he drove her car across the darkened city to the museum to get his car. Cynthia had said she would enjoy the walk back later in the day. Windshield wipers clearing away what was now only a mist as he drove out of the city, he kept the windows open, the soft, moist air cleansing guilt from his soul.

Cynthia had been right about some of the nicer parts of growing older; perhaps enjoying a pleasant interlude was one of them. He'd already survived a heart attack, frequent colonoscopies, deep teeth cleaning, and acid reflux - all part of the ritual of aging and the ignominy of deterioration.

He had learned the most important lesson in life: when you die, you're alone. Somebody can hold your hand, people can cry, worry, and whisper encouragement to you, but they're not going with you. Death is the opposite of life - the antithesis of together. Maybe, after you cross the great divide, parents, relatives, ancestors, God, and figures in white robes meet you - but you must cross that divide alone. Nobody flies into the light with you. Having one more good memory before the great alone was not so bad. Perhaps he should feel a little guilty, but not terrible.

When Adam turned into the gravel driveway in front of the old house, one hundred degree heat had replaced the mist-softened morning of eastern Nebraska. He prepared to climb the stairs leading to the epicenter of his youthful fears and enter the room where the crazy woman stayed, this time knowing two skeletons were on the bed.

He was so preoccupied with his fears that the femur lying on the top step didn't register in his consciousness. It wasn't until he bent down to pick it up that he realized something was wrong. Only four possibilities existed to explain why it was there, and three of them were unlikely. The skeletons had walked away and one had lost a bone during the stroll; the crazy woman from the closet had thrown the bones around; a mouse big enough to drag a human thighbone was loose in the house; or someone had been there and discovered his grisly secret.

The only weapon he could find was the bone, and he gripped it as if it were a macabre bat. Though brittle and light with age, it was still better than nothing. Adam crept silently towards the room, peering around the corner as if he were a television cop looking for bad guys. Whoever had been in the house was gone, and so were any hopes of learning more from the bones.

Anger and hatred had attacked the skeletons, adding one more chapter of inhumanity to the souls they had once been. The brother and sister from California, if that was who they once were, had been as destroyed in death as they had been in life. Someone, or something, had crushed their skulls and rib cages. The only bone he could find unbroken was the femur in his hand. Chunks, shards, and even powder covered the floor. The silver and turquoise jewelry lie on the floor in pieces, as if flattened by a lunatic's hammer.

This hadn't been the work of the crazy woman he'd always thought hid in the room, but it was done by someone just as demented. Real flesh and blood and not the imagination of a frightened child had destroyed the skeletons.

"Why?" He asked as if the house could answer. "Why would anyone do this? How could some bones, buried for almost a century, cause such violence and destruction? It couldn't have been my brother. He might have thought I'd lost my mind and try to have me committed for smuggling skeletons, but he wouldn't have done this."

Suddenly Adam knew the answer, and began talking to the people the remains had once been. "They knew who you were, and I believe I do too. I think you were friends of my grandmother. I think one of you was that young woman in the picture and the other is her brother. You came out here to help care for my dad. But what did you do to deserve this? What could you have done to make someone hate you so much that they would destroy your bones eighty or ninety years after you were dead? What's next. . ."

Fragments of window glass cutting into Adam's face and the sound of a bullet slamming into the oak closet interrupted his conversation with the piece of skull in his hand.

Lying prone on the floor, hands covering his head, he was as incapable of action as the human remains scattered around the room. When the second shot blew out the remaining glass in the window and left a large hole in the plaster wall within a foot of where he was lying, Adam rolled under the old bed and clasped his hands to his burning face, amazed by the amount of blood on his palms and fingers when he pulled them away.

He stayed under the bed long after someone yelled something about "all son-of-a-bitches going to hell" as a noisy truck raced away behind the trees.

CHAPTER TEN

EVERYTHING THEY OWNED WAS IN THE WAGON. THE broken-down, rib-showing mules pulling it were barely able to stand, let alone walk. It had been three weeks since Molly Roberts had rousted the remaining members of the formerly notorious gang out of their shanty on the edge of the South Dakota badlands, and she wasn't going to let them stop for anything.

Molly was taking the six surviving members of the Roberts gang, the most fearsome, straightest shooting, rootingest-tootingest wild bunch in the Old West, to a better life on her firstborn son's ranch. George would take them in, she'd said. He had to.

With every mile across the prairie, dodging settlements and farms, Molly cursed the hard times. The past ten years had been rough due to all sorts of newfangled inventions like telephones, radios, and automobiles. She and the others had never outgrown their propensity to live high off other folks' livestock. Except that those damned creations, including miles of barbed wire, had brought an end to their way of life.

The west just wasn't wild anymore, not as it had been when she was the hard-riding wife of Charlie Roberts, the West's most fearsome outlaw. She and the boys could no longer drive stolen stock for days across open range. Hordes of immigrant farmers had put up fences and planted wheat and corn on the gang's get-away trails.

Molly figured their luck had finally taken a turn for the better when Autie, her youngest son and the only one of the bunch who knew his letters, had read them an article in a newspaper about George Roberts. The rest of the gang knew him as the little bastard who'd abandoned his family and took off on their best horse ten years earlier. The article stated that George had been elected president of the Medicine Lodge Cattlemen's Association.

Autie had stolen the paper, taken it back to the shack, and read it out loud. He'd followed each word with his finger to make sure he didn't lose his place and read how his long-lost brother was some big hero. He'd gotten a ranch for helping some dead kid stupid enough to get gored by a range cow.

"Now thet's good luck, and thet's my boy. I know he'll be a wanting to take care of his momma and what's left of his kin. We're a going to see my boy," Molly had told the others. Rising off the stump she used as a stool in the shack they'd built in a blind corner of an almost impenetrable canyon, she had started throwing her meager possessions into linen sacks. "Come on," she chided the others. "We got ourselves a long trail to be a-riding, all the way down to the other side of the Platte. Autie, you be taking yer pony over to the injuns and swap 'er fer a couple a mules. Vern, tend the old wagon; make her suitable fer this trailing. It be the last we be needing of thet old wreck. Ain't no daylight to be a wasting. We be out a here 'fore sundown and be a camping on the trail."

The bunch hadn't had to do much arranging to make sure all their belongings fit in the broken-down old Conestoga. They had little to pack, considering their years of hiding from the angry warriors of the Ogallala Sioux, their closest neighbors and most frequent victims of their felonious activities.

The size of a child and dressed like man, trudging across the prairie beside the spavined animals pulling their belongings, Molly wondered if George would recognize her. Age, poor nutrition, life on the run, and extreme poverty since the death of her husband had worked her over cruelly. It had been forty-two years since her birth to an Indian trader along the Yellowstone, and she looked every day of it, plus a bunch more.

She wasn't trekking to Nebraska out of undying motherly love for her firstborn. That emotion was for fools who lived in town and had never seen bad times. She was going because George owed her. It was as simple as that. She'd damn near died birthing him in that sorry bunch of cottonwoods on the Arkansas while federal marshals from the Indian Nations were beating the bushes for their bunch. She had been alone - her husband trailing stolen horses down to Mexico to sell - and that kid had almost split her in half. She still felt the pain. Now it was time for him to repay his momma for bringing him into the world where he could become such a big shot.

He could take care of her and the younger brother he hadn't stayed around long enough to get to know, as well as his father's brother and family. Besides, maybe there would be rich enough pickings down that way that they could revive the family business. The last time they'd worked along the Medicine Lodge had been back in the eighties, before George had burst out of her, squealing and carrying on.

Bands of Indians traveling between reservations in worn out wagons or with a few poor horses piled high with packs and kids were common sights on the North Table. George Roberts always tried to help the poor red men whenever he could. Probably, he'd once explained to Sarah, because he knew what it was like to be down-and-out and hunted by the law and soldiers.

He and his two ranch hands had just finished branding and cutting their bull calves, throwing the bloody testicles into a bucket so they could have a Prairie Oyster feed that night. A keg of beer was cooling in ice that George had shipped out from North Platte for the party when he saw the wagon slowly rolling across the prairie.

Jumping onto Captain Jack, the fastest stallion he owned, George rode out to greet the small band of travelers, intending to invite them to camp in his trees and have some of the oysters. They had more of the delicacies than he and his hands could eat, and most would just spoil in the summer heat anyway.

The young rancher knew the immigrants weren't Indians as soon as he was close enough to make out the starving mules barely able to place one hoof in front of the other. Red men would take better care of their stock, he thought. Sure, the Sioux might eat their animals if need be, but he'd never seen them let horses or mules suffer as those poor beasts were.

He didn't have time to rebuke the bunch of chicken thieves, as he referred to anyone who raised his ire. He'd picked up the saying from his father who had thought stealing horses a noble occupation while thieving chickens from poor folks the most unworthy. He immediately recognized the voice that issued from the small lump of rags sitting on the wagon seat next to the kid driving the mules.

"Georgie, my boy! Is thet you? I missed you so. I reckoned you'd been took by savages and reared as a redskin 'til I seen yer name in the paper. Come on now, give yer mama a hug and be saying hello to yer brother Autie. Why, he's gotten his name from the great General Custer hisself."

For the briefest moment, George considered turning Captain Jack around, riding hard back to the house, and locking Sarah, the baby, and himself in the storm cellar. His memories of Molly Roberts were not of a loving mother who would fret and pine for her oldest son. She'd been the toughest of the gang, bossing his father, him, and everyone else around, swearing and carrying on like a regular old cavalry sergeant. His ma had been a terror: hitting, cussing, and complaining about bad breaks - what the world owed her, and why he wasn't a better son. George had always thought his dad would have quit the family business and gone straight if it hadn't been for his ma.

Rejecting his urge to flee, George sat mute on Captain Jack, staring openmouthed at the wagon and its passengers. "George! You be setting there like you don't got no sense. Don't you have nothing to say? Sitting on thet fancy horse like you owned the whole danged world. You be thinking, mayhaps, yer too good for the woman all tore up a birthing such a big ol' fat baby."

"Mama," George was finally able to croak, his voice sounding as it had when a whore in the Medicine Lodge Hotel helped him pass through puberty. "What are you doing here? How'd you find me?" He was angry at himself for the ungracious way he sounded as soon as he blurted out, "What do you want?"

"George. Thet ain't no way to talk to yer poor old mama and her folks. We're all thet's left of yer kin. Yer poor daddy were hung-up like a dog up in Wyoming by a bunch of ranch hands. Why, this poor child right here is yer little brother you never helped grow-up, and looky here, we got li'l children in the back of this broken-down ol' wagon. You gotta help us."

Now George was sure it was his mother, and she hadn't changed one bit. The kind greetings and asking for hugs was over. She'd brought them here to live off him and Sarah, and she wasn't going to make any more bones about it.

"George, Goddammit! You be doing what your ma says," a man he recognized as his father's shiftless brother standing in the back of the wagon yelled at him. "We be living pretty poor off the hog and be needing a hand. You need to be a helping us out. It's yer duty as kin. Yer poor little cousins back here be so excited about meeting you they be a peeing their pants jest to get here. Now they be a starving and yer sitting there all high and mighty."

"And I'll work hard fer you Georgie. I'll be a top hand, just like my big brother. I can rope and shoot and ride with the best of 'em. Put me to work, and I'll pay my own way," yelled the boy holding the reins.

At least the kid said he would work. George considered that a good start. The boy had sand, even if the rest didn't. Blond, blue-eyed and strapping for his age, a good-natured, hardworking brother might be just what the place needed.

George knew there was nothing else to say, they were his kin and he had a duty to care for them. Sarah helped him move his mother into the house, giving her the upstairs room with the built-in closet. His brother took a place in the bunkhouse with the three other hands, and his uncle's family turned part of the barn into living quarters.

Though they had moved in without so much as a 'by your leave,' Sarah tried to make them feel at home. "Now, George, don't you worry," she said the next morning as he gulped down bacon and her plate-sized flapjacks. "I'm sure we'll all get along just fine. With Consuelo and Jesus to help, your ma and the others will be no trouble at all."

"I wish I could believe that," he said as he grabbed his rifle from the corner and started out the door, "but as I recall, Mama was even hard for Pa to get along with. Sometimes he'd take off by himself for long spells just to get away from her. I 'spect she'll be a good deal more trouble than you think."

Sara poured herself another cup of coffee from the pot boiling on the huge wood burning stove that took up most of one wall of the kitchen. She watched out the window as her husband and the cowhands raced their horses out of the corral, waving their hats in the wind as they galloped away. Consuelo was playing with the baby in the parlor, and Jesus had just left to gather the eggs. It was a good life, and she wouldn't allow anything or anybody to change it, including her newly discovered mother-in-law.

Years on the run and a childhood among the Blackfeet had ingrained stealth into Molly's nature. Sarah didn't know she was awake until small but strong hands grabbed her shoulders and spun her around. "Now we be alone, let me git a look at you. I 'spect yer jest one of them city gals ain't worth a lick when it comes to a living off the country. Without this fancy house and them Mex servants, you be as worthless as tits on a boar."

"Why Mrs. Roberts," Sarah said, shocked at hearing obscenities in her own kitchen. "I didn't know you were up. Sit down. I'll get you some coffee and anything else you want."

"Coffee, and fix me some of them cakes and cook 'em fer the rest of my bunch, missy. And while you be working, know things be changing around here. My boy George be too danged peculiar as it is. Teaching him to read and write like he were a regular dandy. Keep yer yap shut and don't say nothing to him. Me and the others figure this place be jest fine. We can steal a lot of stock and keep them on his range 'til we drive 'em up to the Sioux. We spied out the trail on the way here.

"I'll be giving the orders now, and you and them two greasers stay outen the way. George'll come 'round, I 'spect, soon as he sees us making money. Now you send that female Mex to get me some decent clothes from somewheres. Have thet other un, thet boy-girl, saddle me a horse so I can look around. And you remember missy, ain't no end to the bad stuff can happen to you or them Mexes. I can raise yer baby jest fine, and George'll join back up with the gang. It's in his blood. Everything will be jest like it always were.

Even when Molly hit Consuelo while ranting about having to share a roof with "two damn greasers," Sarah tried her best to be gracious. Out of fear for her child and the two young Californians, she didn't say anything to George. After all, Molly had lived a hard life, and she'd probably start acting nicer once she grew more familiar with her new surroundings. "That's what I expect will happen and why we will continue being nice to her," she'd told Consuelo and Jesus when they came to her with stories of abuse.

Sarah, Consuelo and Jesus often overheard George's kin planning their return to the outlaw ways while George was out on the range. Every minute they weren't riding around the country, they sat in the parlor demanding someone wait on them hand-and-foot and whispering secretly to one another.

After six months of sudden disappearances, when they started showing up late at night, drunk, wearing new clothes, and one time even riding different horses and armed with new rifles and pistols, Sarah knew they had implemented their nefarious plans. She knew if George ever find out, he would send them away.

Sarah didn't care at all about the adults and thought it would be good riddance to get rid of them, but she knew it would hurt George to send Autie away. He often told her how fond he was of his younger brother and how he looked forward to bringing him into the ranching business as a partner. 'Poor George has suffered enough,' she thought, 'he shouldn't have to run his own brother off his ranch.'

CHAPTER ELEVEN

AUTIE'S NOSE DRIPPED BLOOD AND THE ROPE TORE THE bare skin on his wrists as he struggled to free himself. "You let him go. You let my pa go free," he yelled. "We ain't been stealing yer shitty ol' horses! We jest needed to borrow a couple to git us outen these damned mountains and back home."

Autie was ten, old enough for his pa to have taken him along to the Yellowstone, and he'd held up his end of the bargain. He wasn't going to let these chicken-stealing ranch hands make him cry or see him beg, even if they had hit him in the face a couple of times. They were trying to scare him by acting like they were going to hang his Pa and leave him to fend for himself a thousand miles from home.

Everything had happened so fast. It seemed like just a few minutes ago that Pa had shaken him awake in their camp along the Greybull River about fifteen miles west of Meeteetse, Wyoming, and told him it was time. They'd saddled their horses and traveled quietly along the river until they came to the wooden corral where the rancher kept his prize colts.

They had managed to tie five of them into a string and were nearly off the ranch before that blamed dog started barking and carrying on. They would have still been able to make their getaway too, if only that fool old black bear the dog had been barking at hadn't run right across their trail and scared all their horses silly. The animals had started rearing and bucking, fouling the ropes, squealing like they were being eaten alive. He and his Pa had just managed to get them loose and underway again when these ranch hands showed up shooting off their guns, hitting his Pa in the shoulder, spattering blood all over. Then they knocked him off his horse and tied him up. Now they had his Pa sitting on his horse under a tall ponderosa pine while a big, ugly man was fixing a rope around his neck.

Just as he started to yell out again, the cowboy who'd tied him up like a hog for market kicked him in the leg and yelled back, "Shut yer damn yap, you horse-stealing little sumbitch, or we'll swing you from a branch yer ownself."

"Ow," Autie hollered loud enough for everybody to hear. "Okay. You hurt me and got me scared. Let my Pa go and we'll be on our way. We'll never come back. I promise."

"Now boy." The older man who'd been giving orders to the rest, the one dressed in fancy clothes and wearing a pearl-handled revolver on his gun belt, rode his horse over to Autie and looked down at him. "You need to watch with intensity and ponder long and hard on your providence. Such is the fate that befalls those souls who choose to ride the lawless trail."

Finally convinced this was not a show for his education, Autie darted one way and then jumped the other, escaping from the man holding him down and plunging into the fancy man's beautiful palomino stallion, causing him to rear in alarm. "Please don't kill him. Please let my Pa go." he begged. "I promise we'll leave right away and won't bother your old horses no more. Please. You can't hang him. He's my Pa!"

Still struggling to control his horse, the older man struck Autie across the face with his quirt, bringing a drop of blood to the youth's forehead, and began yelling about a boy respecting his betters. Just then, a low voice, carried above the confusion. Laden with dignity, Charlie Robert's words caused Autie, the ranch owner, and the cowhands to stop and stare. "Boy. Know who you are. You were born a Roberts and that's what you'll die. Remember this day fer the rest a yer life. Don't never cry and don't never beg. Don't do no good, and it ain't what a man does. You take what's coming to you and face it square. When you see yer Ma, tell her I went like a brave man.

"The rest of you can kiss my ass in hell." Then, just as the cowhand who'd placed the hangman's noose over the outlaw's neck swung around to strike him, Charlie Roberts kicked the horse he was sitting on in the ribs and hanged himself.

Autie quickly wiped the tears from his eyes and watched his father swing. He could tell his Pa's neck broke when the horse bolted out from under him. The ten-year-old horse thief stood as straight as he could, vowing that no one would ever again see him cry or hear him beg again.

Silently, as if the outlaw's final epitaph had given them a glance at their own fate, the rancher and his men cut Autie's hands loose, handed him the reins to his pony - the first horse that had ever been only his - and rode away. Standing on the saddle of his small mount, Autie cut the rope around his father's neck and fell to the ground with the body.

He buried his father in a shallow grave beside the river under a stand of aspen and covered the mound with rocks, hoping to prevent wild animals from feasting on the remains. As he slowly rode away, forcing himself not to look back, he had two thoughts: surviving the trip to South Dakota and getting even with the peckerheads who'd strung up his Pa.

———————

Revenge had been easy. The trail out of the mountains took him right past the ranch. He had waited in the trees until after dark and everyone was asleep. Then, he'd thrown a burning kerosene lantern into a mound of hay in the barn that housed the rancher's prize bulls on one side and the ranch hand's bunks on the other.

Autie didn't even turn around to see what destruction he'd caused until he was almost back to Meeteetse. When he finally did, it looked like the entire western sky was glowing red. Proud of himself and sure that he'd not only burned down the ranch, but set the forest on fire as well, he fell asleep along the Greybull River just as the town's fire department roared past with four white horses pulling a small pumper.

He was gone long before the fire crew or anyone else from the ranch rode into town with stories of a destroyed barn, two dead cowhands, and the best breeding stock in Wyoming turned into burned steak. Autie was halfway across the Big Horn Mountains, one hundred miles to the east, before anybody started looking for the brat who might have known something about the fire.

Word spread around the country you could recognize the kid by the paint pony he rode. Only by then Autie was astride a big bay he'd taken from a stable in the small town of Worland. He had set his painted pony loose in the middle of the mountains. He was good enough on the dodge to know nobody was going to catch him.

The long ride from Wyoming to South Dakota had been Autie's greatest adventure. For a ten-year-old, living off the land, hiding from people, staying away from towns and ranches except to steal food, had been just about the most fun in the world. Sure, he'd missed his pony and mourned his Pa, and he hadn't been looking forward to telling his Ma about his father's misfortune because she would blame him, but he had the time of his life.

He had felt a great sense of disappointment when his uncle tried to steal his horse, not knowing it was Autie's at the time. Because of his uncle's botched attempt at thievery, he was back with his Ma and the rest of his poor relation.

Autie had grown up quickly over the next couple of years. At the age of thirteen, he had learned how to read and write when he spent the winter in the mining town of Deadwood - his pay for keeping the coal fires glowing in one of the town's biggest whorehouses. The women had taught him his letters during their off-hours, rewarding him for successful accomplishment with the wares everyone else had to purchase.

When he went back to the badlands the next summer to work in the family rustling business, he could read and write and had sampled all the bordello's goods. Two years later, when his family showed up at George's ranch, Autie figured he was just about the most grown-up, top-hand, ladies man in western Nebraska. Hadn't he killed men in Wyoming, made a ride of close to one thousand miles alone when he was only ten, and pleasured all the ladies in one of Deadwood's finest houses without ever hearing a complaint?

In those days, his confidence had no bounds. He was going to be top hand on George's ranch and work his way up to becoming a trusted partner. Many of the other young men around Medicine Lodge had thought his swagger and the cocky angle he wore his hat to be arrogant and high-handed. For a while, even many of the hardworking farmers of the North Table tired hard to dislike the kid who went around referring to himself as Cowboy George's kid brother, but they couldn't. He was too damn likeable.

Little boys wanted to be just like him, and mothers pushed their daughters in front of him at socials. Rumor had it that he and George were about to buy up most of the land between the Medicine Lodge and the Platte. And almost everybody, even some of the people who didn't like him, thought it would be a lucky girl who caught Autie Roberts.

From the moment he had first seen her, however, Autie had eyes only for the raven-haired young beauty from California who helped care for his nephew. Unfortunately, no matter how hard he tried to win her over, she wouldn't return his affection.

In the spring of 1917, almost two full years after moving onto George's ranch, Autie couldn't stand it any longer. He was the cock-of-the-walk and everybody around Medicine Lodge knew it. He'd grown tired of waiting for Consuelo to fall under his charms. If she gave him a chance, she'd realize how much she loved him. He was man enough, and confident enough, to give her that chance - even if she didn't want it.

Before taking more forceful action, such as throwing her onto a horse and galloping her away to a line shack, he decided to give her one more chance to see the light. He waited until one afternoon when her brother, Jesus, was gathering eggs in the chicken coop to put his plan into motion.

Autie had never paid any attention to the small, slightly built boy before. In fact, he hadn't ever talked to him except to mutter 'Howdy' when they passed. He'd figured the kid was one of those girly-boys because of the way he sashayed about, spending his time with the women in the house instead of out with the men and the horses. That was all right with Autie, as long as he kept his distance from him.

"Hey, Jesus," Autie had said, clapping the boy on the back as if he was an old friend. "How you be a doin'? I ain't seen much of you fer the longest spell and thought I'd be a stopping by to say howdy."

"Hello to you, Señor Autie," the slightly built young man answered, keeping his head down and staring at the floor. "How are you? I did not expect to find you out here with the chickens and poor Jesus. You are always either taking care of the cows or trying to speak to my sister."

Autie tried his best to act casual as he helped fill Jesus' basket with eggs, as though he didn't have an ulterior motive for befriending the young Californian. "Well, it be neighborly to help a pard with his chores sometimes. Yer looking like yer working hard, and I reckoned to lend a hand."

"That's very kind of you, Señor," Jesus whispered, "I see you working hard all the time too, and you're so big and strong."

Autie picked up an egg and acted as if he was carefully examining it for cracks. He figured he had the younger man convinced they would become great friends, and he changed the subject to Consuelo. "Oh by the way, I do be a needing a favor. You know, come a time when you ain't all up to yer neck in chores and all."

He thought it might be better to wait for a while to ask, but he couldn't stand it any longer. "Shucks, I guess now is as right a time as any. I need to talk with Consuelo by our lonesomes, away from the house and Sarah. I be a needing yer help. Hows 'bout setting up a rendezvous fer me?"

The anger in the other boy's voice surprised him. He didn't believe he had done anything to deserve it. He was just trying to find an ally in his heart's quest. "Well, you think you are such a big, strong man," Jesus responded. "Why don't you just ask her? Why bother me with such silly problems. I have no time for it. I have much to do, and I must get these eggs collected."

Autie's answer was equally curt. "'Cause I have asked her, you danged fool, and she ain't agreeable. I'm a needing you to ask her to meet you out by the old wallow tonight, only I'll be there instead. Once I show her how deep my feelings be, maybe you can go on a living here with us cowhands fer a spell."

"Why should I do this for you, Señor Autie? Consuelo is the only family I have left." Jesus set the basket down on the straw floor so hard some of the eggs cracked. "She might hate me and never speak to me again if I pull this trick on her. Then what would happen to poor Jesus? Better I should be sent away than to have my sister despise me."

Autie realized he had overplayed his hand, counting on the timid boy to cower instead of showing steel in his flashing eyes. Not knowing what else to do, he opened his soul. "I'll tell her I made you do it. Don't fret 'bout that none. I'll say I forced you to help me out. Said I'd run you off'n the ranch if you didn't. Please. I'll make her believe me. She'll know it be true 'cause I love her so much. Please, you gotta help me. I don't know what I'll do if I can't have her."

"Okay. I will help you," Jesus finally replied. "I will watch the wallow after dark. When I see you flash a lantern, I will tell her to meet me there. She will find you instead," he said, shrugging off Autie's attempt to shake his hand.

Jesus rushed to the room he shared with his sister that Sarah had divided by hanging sheets from hooks on the ceiling. He fell onto his bed shaking with sobs. He had always known he was different from other boys, preferring to dress in his sister's clothes and putting on her make-up and perfume to playing outside.

Consuelo had known he was different before he did, and when everybody else was in bed, she treated him as though he was her beautiful little sister: painting his nails, fixing his hair and dressing him in her clothes as if he was a doll. She always told him he was beautiful when he wore her dresses and make-up, and he looked enough like her to be her twin.

The secret he carried in his heart was that he had fallen in love with the dashing young cowhand who had had just asked him to arrange a date with his sister. He had thought his heart would burst when Autie announced his love for Consuelo instead of him. So many times he had tried to make eye contact with Autie, had even openly flirted with him, trying everything he could to be noticed. He had to do something to win the cowboy he loved so much.

After dinner he asked Consuelo for her help, not telling her what he was about to do. She dressed him in her finest gown, placed her silver comb in his hair, and told him he was the most beautiful señorita in the world. As she left to tend the baby, she cautioned him to stay in their room, away from the window. His beauty was their secret and not to be shared with anyone else. "Maybe it will be different," she whispered, "when we are back in Los

Angeles, but out here on the prairies, it will be terrible for both of us if anyone finds out."

Jesus wanted the same as Autie - a chance to show his love. If he did, perhaps, he would return his affection. By the time Autie knew his lover was not Consuelo, it would be too late. The dashing cowboy would finally discover it was Jesus he loved.

The moon was only a small sliver on the edge of the sky as Jesus stole out the back door. Even though millions of stars were twinkling in the heavens, they offered little light. He couldn't see the ground in front of his feet as he slowly walked out to the wallow after the flashing lantern signaled Autie was waiting.

Wearing Consuelo's high heels on the uneven prairie was far more difficult than on the smooth floor of their bedroom. He fell off the back steps and stumbled with every step. Though his heart urged him to hurry, he dared not. Autie would be expecting Consuelo's grace and dignity, not somebody staggering around in the dark as the drunken ranch hands did every Saturday night.

"Consuelo, thet be you?" the man he loved called through the darkness. "I know yer specting Jesus 'stead of me, but let me speak. When you see how deep my love is, you'll thank them stars you came."

Autie reached out to the beautiful young woman, lightly placing his hands around her waist, guiding her into his arms. "Oh Autie," she moaned, her satin voice catching in passion. "I have waited so long for this moment."

To Autie's surprise, Consuelo was the aggressor. The chaste, beautiful young woman he had sought for so long was an uninhibited lover, even more so than the soiled doves in Deadwood. Her passion exceeded his. While he'd hoped she would share a shy kiss with him once he spoke of his love for her, he was soon under a spell cast by her hands, lips, and tongue. Before he could even speak of love, long before he would have gathered the courage to touch her, his manhood was in her mouth, going French as the whores called it, something he supposed proper young women such as Consuelo had never even heard of before.

Afterwards, Consuelo held him in her arms, covering his face with kisses once again, urging him to sleep. Physically satisfied, full of love for this beautiful young woman he would soon marry and lying in her arms, the soft night air of the plains lured him to sleep. Dozing off he murmured, "I love you Consuelo. I have since I first laid eyes on you. If this be only a dream, I hope I never wake up."

He fell asleep with her soft words, "It is not a dream, my darling. I am here with you. Go to sleep, my sweet."

Autie awoke alone the following morning just as the rising sun cast pink rays on the eastern horizon. Pants still unbuttoned, he barely had time to dress and wash away the smell of Consuelo's rose-scented perfume before George and the other two hands showed up to begin the morning chores. "Oh. I just decided I'd sleep out on the trail. Like we done in the days on the run," he told them when they asked why they hadn't seen him in the bunkhouse.

Two days later, just after lunch, the morning's rain turned to a fine mist blown hard enough by a cold north wind to sting exposed skin. Autie left the house after speaking with his mother, more confused than he'd ever been in his life. Consuelo had acted as if she barely knew him, as she had always done before the night they spent together. She had been polite but distant. He had kept searching her face for a smile, a twinkle in her eye, a spark of love, but saw nothing. She had gushed over the baby, hugged Sarah, and seemed positively enamored with George, but she'd treated him with contempt and acted as if he wasn't even there.

He stood on the porch and buttoned his heavy coat before wading through the mud to get to the bunkhouse where the boys had a fire and a game of cards going. Jesus hurried through the door and whispered in his ear. "Consuelo says for you to meet her in one hour in the high loft in the barn. She says you must be quiet so your aunt and uncle do not hear. She will be there waiting for you."

The boy, as Autie thought of him, even though he was only three years younger, was gone before he could say thank you. He hurried to the bunkhouse, trying to think of an excuse why he had to clean up and couldn't play poker. His heart was bursting. Within in hour he would be in the arms of his love. If she'd wanted to act like she didn't know him in the house, he guessed it was all right. But she was going to have to quit playacting real soon.

He would ask her to marry him that afternoon. Then they would not have to sneak around. George and Sarah already loved her and would be proud to have her as a sister-in-law. He'd convince his Ma and uncle to quit stealing or go away. He was going to marry the love of his life and be a partner in the biggest ranch on the North Table.

The light in the loft was as dim as it had been out by the wallow, and Consuelo was as passionate and as much in a hurry as she'd been the first time. Autie had thought this would be a romantic encounter, filled with soft words and tender caresses, eliciting from her a promise of marriage, babies, and a wonderful life together. But he was soon lying back in her arms as he had before, spent, and a little confused by her haste.

"My darling Consuelo," Autie finally murmured after the passion had dissipated into glorious feelings of love, sparking a tenderness he had never felt before. "I knew you could have strong feelings fer me. We're gonna tell folks today." "Do not speak yet, my love. We have our whole lives to talk of such. Just lie here a little longer before we part," Consuelo whispered into his ear, brushing his lips with long, slender fingers.

Autie's heart would break if she ever treated him again as she had that morning, and he couldn't keep such a wonderful secret any longer. She had to spend the entire afternoon with him, and then they would announce their betrothal at dinner. Grabbing her fingers firmly but tenderly, taking them from his lips and speaking with the pride he would have as her husband, he told her of his plans. "Now girl, there be no sense keeping it quiet. I'd be plumb surprised if Sarah and George ain't already guessing where you disappeared to this afternoon and the other night. I reckon I couldn't stand it fer you to act like you don't know me again. We'll just stay here awhile and then tell 'em we're gonna marry up. You don't have nothing to worry about ever again."

Autie had expected joy, maybe she was too cultured to shriek with happiness, but he never imagined she would meet his expression of love with softly falling tears that quickly became sobs. "Here now," he reassured her. "I don't know why yer a sobbing but ain't nothing bad gonna happen. I love you and you love me. If it's my Ma yer afeard of, don't be. I'll set her right down and tell her how it is. Don't cry. There ain't nothing to cry about. Honest!"

When she shrugged off his embrace and crept farther into a corner, he was ready to assume the role of understanding male. "I guess you just need a time to git used to the idea of finally being Mrs. Autie Roberts. Why thet's okay. You run along and get all fixed up. I be right down myself. Then we'll tell all my kin."

"No! No! You must not tell anybody," came her stricken reply as she sprang to the ladder. "We can never tell anyone. I am pledged to marry a young vaquero in California, and I must be a virgin when I return to him. That is why you cannot touch me and why we cannot tell anyone. Promise you will only be my love here on the prairies." Not waiting for a reply, the beautiful young woman slid down the ladder as quickly as her skirt would allow.

Autie was too stunned to try to stop her. He couldn't move. The horrible news of her engagement to another rampaged through his mind until he heard her scream when she lost her grip on a rung and fell onto the carriage George stored in that section of the barn.

The young cowhand was as surefooted on the ladder in the dark as he was on the hurricane deck of a cowpony. No sooner had Consuelo rolled from the carriage and fallen onto the hard-packed floor than he was beside her again, cradling her in his arms and kissing away her tears.

As quickly as she threw her hands up to cover her face, Autie was faster. Pulling the dainty fingers away with his own, he stared in horror, torn between terrible anger and an overwhelming need to vomit. "You ain't Consuelo," he spat, his hands clenched into fists, drawn back and ready to strike. "Yer the boy, her brother, the one supposed to be sending her to me. Goddamn you to hell!"

"Please Autie. Let me explain. I only did it because I love you so much. Please don't hate me," Jesus begged. "Don't you understand? We're just the same as we were in the barn. There's no difference. You think only of Consuelo, but I know you can love me too."

Autie stared at the boy dressed in women's clothes. His anger turned to fear and his fear back to rage. He could think only of himself. No one could ever know what had happened. He wouldn't be able to stay on the ranch if anybody knew. Jesus had become a threat to his existence. As long as the boy was alive, somebody could find out what Autie had done.

Grabbing a rope from a wall peg, Autie placed a loop over the boy's head, working it past his long hair adorned with the silver comb, and then around his neck. When he spoke again, his voice was devoid of any emotion but hatred. "Damn berdache. Yer going to hang yerself now. Guess you couldn't stand being a girl-boy no more. I'll throw this rope over a rafter, and you'll get to the damn ladder and start climbing. Nobody's ever gonna know nothing except you killed yerself. Ain't no way I'm gonna rest easy long as yer breathing. Ain't nobody but yer sister gonna miss an old berdache, and she be going back to California soon as I talk to George."

The young Californian was at the top of the ladder, holding his silver crucifix to his lips, when the barn door swung open and Consuelo rushed in. She held one of George's pistols in both hands - and pointed it squarely at Autie's chest. "You let him down, Señor Autie. Jesus, you take the rope off your neck and climb down here slowly. If you try to stop him, even if you are Señor George's brother, I swear I will kill you."

"Bitch," Autie spat back humiliated, the love he'd thought he felt for her gone, leaving only rage in its place. "You put him up to this, didn't you? What? You be wanting to have a good laugh at the gringos. Yer a damn greaser whore. I should kill yer sorry ass right now."

"No! You are wrong," she explained. "I didn't know what he was doing. I only knew he put on my clothes and went out to the barn. I came here to find him so no one would see him. I saw what you were doing through the window."

"Yer a lying bitch. I don't know why yer doing this, but soon as he gets down, I be telling George so he runs you both off this ranch. There ain't no room here for Mexicans queers."

"No, Señor," Consuelo said, her voice steady. You will tell no one. Who will they believe, you or me? I will tell them you loved Jesus and are angry only because I found him in your arms and made you stop. If I do, everyone will say you are a *maricon*, a man who loves other men, maybe even little boys. There will be no place for you on this ranch or any other. People will scorn and laugh at you wherever you go.

"Here is what will happen. You will say nothing to anyone and neither shall Jesus nor I. You have our promise. It is our secret."

As soon as she finished speaking, Autie saddled his horse and rode away across the prairie. He hadn't believed a word she'd said. You couldn't trust a woman who'd whore out her brother. He'd have to figure out a way to ensure their silence.

———

Exactly one week later, George read a wanted poster in Medicine Lodge about a gang of rustlers working the Platte. On the poster was a description of horses and weapons the thieves had taken when they rustled fifty head of cattle. George knew where to find the horses and the guns. The animals were in his corral and the rifles and pistols were in the tack house.

Within an hour of George's return to the ranch, his newly found relatives, including his brother who he had hoped to make a partner, were on their stolen horses riding rapidly out of sight. After throwing their weapons in the wallow where they would rust away, he'd told them to get off his place. "I won't turn you over to the law," he'd said. "But if I ever catch any of you back on this land again, I will. If I ever catch any of you stealing from me, I'll kill you."

He didn't shed a tear over his Ma, for as long as he could remember, there had never been any love lost between them. But what bothered George was Autie's joy at leaving, calling out as he rode away that it was going to be great to be away from queers, whores, and assholes.

CHAPTER TWELVE

LONG AFTER HE HEARD A TRUCK ROAR AWAY, ADAM STAYED under the bed listening for sounds suggesting he was not alone. The farmhouse had grown unearthly quiet again. No boards snapped back into place, no wind whistled through the windows. Still, he loaded the fifty-year-old bolt-action shotgun his brother kept on the porch for shooting skunks and carried it as he searched the rest of the house and the outbuildings.

After cleaning the cuts on his face, Adam anesthetized his shattered nerves with doses of Johnny Walker. He questioned his earlier reaction to the destruction of the bones and the subsequent attempt on his life. It had seemed reasonable to assume both had been efforts to keep him from discovering the identity of a person who had committed murder long before he was born.

"Yeah right!" He said to the man staring back from the mirror in his folk's bathroom as he discarded the detritus of too many scotch and waters into the septic system. "Sure. If they died in 1920, then the murderer has to be over one hundred years old. How likely is that?"

When the guy in the mirror didn't answer, he had to. "There's no way that's possible, you old fool. What's the matter with you?

"So, then, why would somebody want to shoot at a nice guy like me?" Staring straight into his own eyes, remembering how he had gazed into a beautiful woman's from an even closer distance, the scent of her still in his nostrils, he realized his own complicity. Hate had driven the vandalism of the bones and the shooting all right, but recent events had caused the hatred.

A wife of many years having an affair was more than enough to make a gun-happy husband hate the bastard sleeping with her. Cynthia's beer-drinking, misogynistic, good-old-boy husband had gotten loaded, destroyed the bones, and tried to kill him. It was the only explanation that made sense.

Anybody still alive who might have known Jesus and Consuelo Vargas would have to be ancient. Besides, how would anybody know he had dug them up and hid their remains in a bedroom? Except for some people who saw him as they drove by - and probably didn't know who he was - only Cynthia, his brother Jake, and his wife back in Boulder knew he was staying at the farm.

"This is just freaking great. I came over here to find out why I was afraid of the dark as a kid, and now I have crushed bones upstairs and a jealous husband shooting at me. I'm too old for this shit." Talking out loud still helped fill the void he felt in the house. Adam was just about to further berate himself when the phone rang.

"Oh no! What if it's Cynthia's husband? What do I say if he says he knows about us, and he's coming back with his rifle? What do I do?" He had no answer, and he didn't want to talk to anybody anyway. But as the phone kept ringing, his cowardliness embarrassed him. Adam finally picked up the phone and uttered a tenuous, "Hello."

"Hello. Why haven't you called? I've got some great news about my work. You've been ignoring me while you fool around with your ghosts." Glad to hear his wife's voice on the phone, he was relieved to discover nobody had called and told her about his philandering.

But he didn't know if he felt any better than before he had answered. It wasn't the man whose wife he'd slept with. It was the woman he had cheated on. "Hello Julie," Adam said without enthusiasm, hoping she couldn't read his mind two hundred miles away. "How are you? You must have gone back to work. Anyway, that's what it sounds like."

"Yes, I went back yesterday. We're bidding on a new contract, and I'm the lead researcher. I'm so excited!"

Adam hoped her excitement was enough to keep her talking about herself, so she didn't ask anything else about him. "Well, what is it? You'll do wonderful in the lead. What are you working . . ."

"Mosquitoes. West Nile is spreading like fire over here. Boulder needs something to combat the bloodsuckers. You know the city won't allow spraying with any of the known pesticides. My job is to develop a spray kind to all living creatures, except mosquitoes."

"Great! That's just great. Well, I expect you need to get back to work. Have to find a better bug spray and all that. Good-bye then." He figured if he hung up the phone quickly, she would think he was being sensitive to her workload. He just wasn't quick enough. The questions were out of her mouth before he had finished interrupting her.

"Not so fast. How are you? What have you found out about the bodies? Are you ready to drop this foolishness and come back home? I could use some help around the house."

"Uh, I, uh, I guess I need to be honest with you." Adam hoped he would satisfy her curiosity if she knew there was some, but not too much, danger. "Last night somebody shot at the house. I think it was just kids screwing around."

"Shot at the house while you were inside? Just kids screwing around? Adam you get in your car and drive back here this minute! Did you call the police? I bet you didn't, did you? I'll expect you home in three hours."

She hadn't taken the news as well as he had hoped she would. She had sounded angry, almost as if she was afraid she would lose her housekeeper. He was going to have to talk himself out of this one. "Now, dear, listen to me. My friends and I used to shoot at deserted houses all the time when we were kids." Actually, they never had, and he had never heard of anyone doing it before, but she didn't know that. "It was a game, like playing war. There's a tradition of doing that over here. It was nothing, I promise. Anyway, I can't leave yet. I have those bones upstairs that I need to do something with."

"You take them back to the same place you found them, bury them, and then drive home this instant!"

Adam had to be more forceful - he had become obsessed with finding out why someone had murdered two young people on the family farm. He couldn't stop until he had found the answers, and he wasn't in any hurry to get back and do housework. "Look, I'll tell you what. I'll stay in a motel in Sidney. It'll be safer there. That will give me a chance to do a little more research. I'm close to the answers. I think I know who they were and maybe who killed them."

She couldn't be less interested and had already made up her mind. "Adam, I don't like this. What if they had shot you? What if you were lying up in that old house dead? It might be weeks before anyone found you."

"Now why would anybody purposefully shoot at me?" Of course he knew the answer but he couldn't tell her. "It had to be just a couple of kids screwing around."

Julie had dedicated her life to the scientific method, she worked from knowledge and empirical evidence, not supposition and emotion. With only the limited information he had given her, she had no reason to believe anyone wanted him dead. Besides, he knew she wanted to get off the phone and back to work. If he talked long enough she would concede.

"Oh, all right," she finally muttered. "You stay in Sidney. There is no reason for anybody to want to kill you. If you say that happens there all the time, then that must be it. But be careful from now on!

"Now tell me. Who do you think the remains were, and who killed them?"

Adam told her about his trip to Lincoln, most of it anyway, about his long hours of research in the state museum of history, and about the two young people who had traveled from California to help care for his father. When he got to the part about the Klan, she became fascinated. She hung up after he promised to stay in a motel with rooms only accessible through an indoor hallway so a sniper couldn't shoot him as he unlocked the door.

Adam couldn't call the police. He didn't need them stumbling across the skeletons. If they did, his family's history would become a nationwide high-interest story carried by all major newsgroups. He also didn't want the media discovering the shooter was a jealous husband - a story more harmful to him, even if it was of less interest to the general public.

He became even more convinced who the culprit had been when he found a six-pack of empties where the truck had parked in a gully on the other side of the trees. Judging by the footprints, Cynthia's husband and two of his friends had been drinking beer and having a big time before shooting at him.

Forensic science probably could have proven beyond a doubt who owned the truck and whose fingerprints were on the cans, but he had no reason to look any further. Being cuckolded had been the cause of many murders in history. Adam had almost been another victim of love gone astray.

He walked around to the front door of the house expecting to find footprints in the loose dirt covering the sidewalk that matched those he'd found by the beer cans. He had only used the back entrance, as his family had always done. The front door opened into the parlor, a room reserved for visitors with clean clothes.

The intruders' footprints should have shown up in the dirt as bear tracks did in the snow, except for the thousands of cottontail rabbits who had held a convention on the walk that morning and had almost wiped out any prints made earlier. It wasn't until he got down on his hands and knees that he made out several pairs of shoe prints entering and leaving the front door. Whoever had made one set had shuffled his feet, not lifting his shoes off the dirt as he walked. Adam was sure he used a cane. There was a round mark about the size of a fifty cent piece stamped into the dirt beside each right footprint.

He still felt guilty about sleeping with Cynthia and thought it best he stayed away from her, but he needed to find out which of her husband's friends shuffled his feet and walked with a cane.

"None! And he doesn't know anything about you anyway, so quit worrying." A whimsical smile had flitted across her face when he walked into the museum and asked her. "He's too busy drinking beer with the boys to have spied on us in Lincoln. Why do you think he knows anyway?"

Feelings of guilt aside, she looked wonderful, and he started thinking about the last time they had been together - until he remembered why he was there. "Because a bunch of good old boys crumbled almost every bone of the skeletons to dust and then sat out in the trees drinking beer and taking pot shots at me. I guess there must have been a shortage of rats at the dump."

Her reaction was the same as his wife's had been, only accompanied by hugs and tender kisses. "My God! Are you hurt? You've got to get out of here. Go back home where nobody's trying to kill you!"

Adam had just been through this conversation. Convincing the woman he was having an affair with that he needed to stay should be easier than convincing the scientist in Boulder who wanted him home so he could do housework while she was keeping the country safe from West Nile virus. "Cynthia! Think about it! It couldn't have been anybody but your husband and his friends. I'm going to be careful and stay at a motel in Sidney. But what about you? Has he said anything or threatened you?"

"I told you it wasn't him." she replied, her voice tinged with a hint of frustration. "John and his buddies held their annual wild game banquet in Oshkosh last night. A restaurant shuts down for everybody except them and their families, and cooks all the game they bring with them. I was with him and fifty other people from the time I got home at two in the afternoon until almost three this morning. When did the shooting happen?"

"At 6:30 last evening." Adam had looked at his watch while he was hiding under the bed. "But if it wasn't your husband, my first impression must have been right. It had to have been somebody who knew Jesus and Consuelo when they were alive. It couldn't have been the person who killed them, could it?"

"Oh, how could that be?" Cynthia asked, taking him by the hand and leading him over to a counter where a coffeemaker held a fresh pot.

Adam added powdered cream to the cup she had poured for him while she fixed her own. When they were both sitting down, she in the desk chair and he in the wood chair in front, she answered her own question. "It's impossible for anybody who knew the brother and sister to have shot at you. One of my jobs has been to interview all the senior citizens around here. The oldest one, Robert McDraegor, you remember him, passed away at the age of 101 last March, so I'm sure it wasn't him.

"I've thought about researching it. There's an alarming lack of elderly people over the age of eighty-five in this community. I don't know what happened, but we've had a high mortality rate among that age group. I don't think anybody any younger could have killed those people, if we're correct about the date of their deaths."

"But you should have seen the violence inflicted on those bones. It looked personal."

Cynthia blew over her coffee to cool it. "That is strange, my dear, but two minutes ago, you were ready to convict my husband who somehow found out I slept with you. Now you think the drive-by shooter was one hundred-years old. Maybe, if you stop and think about it, you'll think of a better explanation, such as a bunch of drunken high school students."

"Unless you know any teenagers that walk with a cane and go around yelling about 'son-of-bitches' going to hell, I don't see how that could be."

"Adam, it's been too long since you spent time with bored high school kids on the plains of Nebraska. They drink beer, drive around in pickups, shoot at almost anything that moves and a lot that doesn't, and at any one time there's a couple of kids in town with broken legs or torn up knees from sports walking around with crutches or a cane. Some of them keep using the cane long after they don't need it anymore just because it's cool. If we walk over to the café, I can point out a few to you right now."

His head was spinning. He felt as if he had entered the Twilight Zone. Politely asking Cynthia not to talk for a couple of minutes so he could think, Adam closed his eyes, leaned back in the chair, and considered everything that had happened since he came back to Medicine Lodge.

He still didn't know if the madwoman in the farmhouse was a figment of his fears or a ghost. He had dug up a tomb under his mother's lilacs and found two skeletons, adding two new ghosts, or fears, to his problems. He thought he might know who the dead bodies had been, but he had no idea why they were killed, who buried them, or who knew about it. He did know, however, that somebody cared enough about them to turn their bones into fertilizer, and for the first time in this marriage, he had slept with another woman. She was right in front of him, he wanted to do it again, and he felt guilty about it.

On top of all this, somebody had shot at him and when he told his girlfriend, she reacted the same way his wife had. Except she decided the kids he had made up in a lame attempt to convince his wife it hadn't been a personal attack was exactly who it had been.

His head spinning, he stood up and started to leave. As he was almost to the door, Cynthia caught up with him and breathed a soft, sweet kiss in his ear, whispering, "I'll be at your motel about nine. If you don't want to see me, don't be there. I'll take my broken heart and go home."

Then she pushed him out the door grinning from ear to ear. Adam didn't know if she was happy or laughing at him.

CHAPTER THIRTEEN

ADAM DROVE BACK TO THE FARM FEELING MORE LIKE A socially inept, hormonally challenged teenager than a sixty-year-old. He was no longer concerned about who'd done the shooting. The primary issue clouding his mind was much simpler. Did he want to be in his motel room when Cynthia showed up or not? She had convinced him it was his call. They could be friends, or lovers, or never see each other again. If he met her in his room at nine o'clock that night, he would be taking a conscious, premeditated action. Cynthia Schmidt would become his lover by his choice; it would be impossible for him to claim she had seduced him or he had lost his way in the heat of passion.

When Adam parked by the back door he was exhausted from the war raging in his psyche. He had to find a way to shut-off his mind, and the only method he could think of, besides finishing off his booze and falling asleep, was complete absorption in something else, preferably hard work. He had pledged to give Jesus and Consuelo a burial in a pleasant place with a marker. They deserved better than internment beneath a steel cap as if their existence had shamed the world.

He found an antique steamer trunk with leather handles and hardwood rails on each side to protect its blue and green metal skin stuffed with grease rags next to his brother's tractor. It once must have held someone's dreams. Even battered and gouged, it would make a perfect coffin for the brother and sister. He would bury their remains together in the shade of the tall cottonwood tree growing beside the wallow.

The soil under the tree proved much easier to shovel than he had thought it would. Within an hour, the trunk and its contents were four feet below the surface of the earth. A plain, white cross stood two feet high between the grave and the tree which served as a sentry, guarding the resting place of lives snuffed out too early. After whispering a silent prayer for Jesus and Consuelo, Adam sat next to the grave and thought about his morality - and mortality.

He'd hoped the physical labor of placing the remains into the earth where they could rest for eternity would free his mind of the battle over Cynthia. It hadn't. Was it better for him to have her in his life or not? If his wife and her husband never knew, would the affair still hurt them? On the other hand, they were senior citizens for God's sake! They ate cheap meals at cafeterias frequented by their age group. Nobody was going to wither away and die if they got caught.

Mentally and physically tired from the somber work of burial, Adam fell asleep under the tree and started dreaming. He saw two young people running across the prairie towards him, long dark hair billowing behind them, each wearing a garland of flowers. He believed them to be young lovers until he recognized Consuelo from her picture and realized they were the brother and sister he had just placed into the ground.

He was viewing a scene from the early years of the century. Except for the jet contrails standing out starkly against the brilliant sky, little had changed since the brother and sister had lived on this land with his grandparents. They ran through deep grass on forty acres his family had never plowed under. As far as he could see, native grasses blew in the wind as waves did on the Pacific Ocean that Jesus and Consuelo had known as children.

Laughing and holding hands, they ran to him, the sound of their mirth chasing the breeze. They appeared to recognize him, reaching out in welcoming gestures as if they had expected him. Consuelo, wearing an ankle-length white dress with short sleeves and a high collar, dropped to her knees and began speaking in lightly accented tones, her voice resonating with beauty.

"Señor Adam, Jesus and I knew you would come and take us from that terrible place. We are so happy here on the prairie where we are free to run and love."

As Consuelo spoke, Jesus edged closer, his expression hardening. He was holding the ornate stiletto, which, along with Consuelo's comb that she was wearing, he had placed in the box with their bones. When he spoke, anger edged his voice. "You must avenge us, Señor Adam. That is why you are here. The one who did this must pay for these evil deeds. We did not deserve to die at another's hands.

"Consuelo was going to marry her lover in California and become a great lady and have many beautiful babies. She would have been rich and have lived in a great hacienda looking over the ocean. And I, her most faithful brother, would have had many paramours and lived in her great casa. I would have been a famous poet. Students from all over the world would have come to learn from Jesus.

"You must discover the truth. The Señora has suffered too much. You must end her pain."

"I will do all I can, but who . . ." As he spoke, they begin to disappear. "Wait, please," he begged. "You can't go yet. Who did this? Who has suffered too much?" But they had already transformed from solid to ethereal forms; he could see their shapes, and he could see the clouds at the edge of the horizon through them. Then they were gone, although he was sure the air shimmered with light and movement where they had been.

Adam jerked awake, still pleading with them to stay, more confused than ever about the causes of his childhood trauma. The visit from the young Californians lie at the heart of his being. Was their appearance in the field just another dream, a figment of his terrors, a product of an over-active imagination that had created a crazy old woman with a big knife when he was a child, or were they ghosts? Was the woman in the house also a spirit who had been trying to communicate with him? Had the dead selected him to end their suffering, or was he still merely the carrier of a little boy's terrors?

Who had suffered enough? At first Adam was sure Jesus had meant Consuelo, but he had suffered as much as she. Maybe he meant 'they had suffered enough.' But hadn't their suffering ended when they died? Who was still suffering?

He knew several things for sure. He could repeat verbatim what each had said, and he was going to write it down as soon as possible. Since their images were not fading as dreams usually do, he could describe them in enough detail to have their portraits painted. He would only have to describe one of them to the artist. The brother and sister looked exactly alike.

The sky was deep blue, the sun unhindered by clouds, yet the temperature felt unseasonably cool. If he hadn't known better, he would have sworn it was February and a cold front sliding down from Saskatchewan held the plains hostage. Both the sun and he were failing. It wasn't hot enough for late June, and he wasn't close to discovering why a horrible tragedy had taken place on his grandfather's ranch.

Adam had already searched the house and outbuildings. Besides, his brothers and he had lived there for years. If there had been anything to find, they would have discovered it long ago. On countless days, they had searched for buried treasure, hidden by either pioneers or pirates. They had found old coins, arrowheads, rocks, and discarded farming paraphernalia, but never anything to suggest murder had happened where they lived.

Still, he felt as if he were letting Consuelo and Jesus down; he had to search harder. Then cutting through his despair, he had a slapping-himself on the forehead moment, wondering how his parents had raised such a stupid son. He hadn't looked in the tomb!

Rock walls measuring twelve by twelve - one hundred and forty-four square feet covered with half-inch thick steel - seemed large and excessively protected for a grave under a bunch of lilac bushes. Why would a pit dug for a grave have a space cut out for a door? The answer was obvious. It wouldn't.

Ten minutes of digging under the now blazing sun gained little except for providing an opportunity to think. He didn't have to dig out the tomb. He only needed to remove the roof. The metal consisted of three by twelve sheets someone had welded together after placing them on the foundation. Even permanently joined into one-piece, the sheeting wasn't anything his brother's old WD-9 International diesel tractor couldn't slide.

By good fortune, a long bolt fastened securely with a nut and washer protruded two inches above the steel. The tractor, hooked to a log chain wrapped around the bolt, pulled the metal easily to the side. When he jumped down from the diesel, the hard-packed earthen floor of what had obviously been a residence appeared before him.

Whoever had turned it into a grave had buried the contents of the room as well as the bodies. Shelving littered the floor. Shattered and unbroken bottles lie scattered around. Among the debris was a calendar opened to August 1920: September, October, November, and December had waited patiently for more than eighty years for their turn to be on display.

It would take days to account for everything strewn across the earthen floor, and most of it would probably wind up in Cynthia's museum. He didn't have the time or patience to begin a codification process - not until he found out who had killed Consuelo and Jesus and why fate had condemned them to a hidden grave.

The bone handle of a knife sticking out of an old piece of oilcloth was unmistakable. So were the stains on the white cloth wrapped around the twelve-inch blade. He'd bet anything a modern laboratory would identify the black smudges as human blood. Sure that he held the murder weapon in his hands, Adam began searching for anything else that would aid his search for the truth.

One of his grandfather George's favorite expressions had been, "if it was a snake it would have bit you." He'd meant that you were within a serpent's strike of what you were seeking. Adam had walked past the black, square object sticking out of a back corner of the tomb time after time in his haste to discover clues. He had thought it to be only a piece of dark stone such as those scattered across the floor, but stooping to examine what must have been a doorway leading into the basement of the house, he accidentally brushed it with his hand. Loose rocks clattered to the floor, exposing four leather-bound books, each the size of a small Bible. In graceful, flowing script, the first page of the one on top read: *The Journal of Sarah Lyle: Life and Times on the Plains.*

He felt as if he had just found the Holy Grail. Cradling the journals and the knife against his chest as though protecting sacred artifacts from infidels, he rushed back into the farmhouse and threw himself into the chair his father had been sitting in when he passed into eternal rest one Sunday morning after breakfast.

Adam began reading. While each entry was exciting, especially for someone interested in history, he tried to zero in on anything his grandmother had written that would provide the answers he was seeking. Some entries, however, were too fascinating to ignore.

CHAPTER FOURTEEN

The Journal of Sarah Lyle: Life and Times on the Plains.

AUGUST 10, 1908. AS I HAVE JUST RECEIVED NOTICE OF MY employment to tutor children of the Medicine Lodge Cattle Company on the western plains of Nebraska, I have decided to record my adventures in a journal. I will have the responsibility of furthering the education of five children who are sons and daughters of the owners and the ranch manager. The telegram notifying me of my employment instructed me to go to the Los Angeles Union Pacific Depot where I would find a ticket waiting in my name. I leave next Monday, August 16, 1908.

August 13, 1908. The past few days have been an absolute whirlwind of endeavor. What does one wear while teaching little children in the wilds, and what does one wear on the prairie when one is not?

The choice of suitable clothing is made even more difficult by stories I have heard since my friends learned of my great adventure. Alice told me there are wild Indians on the plains just waiting to kidnap me away and force me to be one of their wives, enduring a life of cutting up buffaloes and being ravished by savages. Jeremiah said he had read that Nebraska gets so cold in the winter one woman died of frozen lungs just walking out to the privy. He said it must have been just dreadful. Her lungs became one terrible piece of ice, neither accepting nor giving off air.

Annie said the summer is so hot and dry that I should surely be the size and color of an African pygmy the next time she saw me. According to her professors, the pygmies used to be quite tall and beautiful light-skinned people until the heat drained their bodies of natural moisture and turned them into tiny, black people.

I have decided to pack my clothes into two trunks, one I just purchased. It is a lovely blue and green with leather handles and wooden boards attached to the sides to keep it from being damaged in travel. This trunk shall become my hope chest while I wait for a wondrously handsome Galahad to ride up on his charger and fall in love with me forever. We shall live in his great castle and have many children. I shall be the queen of the land.

<u>August 20, 1908</u>. I have finally arrived at the headquarters of the Medicine Lodge Cattle Company and am alone in my room after a supper of half-bloody meat, home-baked bread, beans, and rhubarb pie. I am told the fare varies little, except the bloody meat is sometimes burned, and sometimes in a stew. Bread, beans, pie, strong coffee, and stacks of meat are the staples of the diet here, except for breakfast, which always consists of more meat, eggs, and flapjacks. I think I might pine away for Consuelo's chilies and tortillas. Prairie food is not half as exciting as hers, I think.

The train ride was most uncomfortable, even though the ticket did provide me with small sleeping quarters. The engines were dreadfully noisy and smoke billowed everywhere. The magnificent scenery, however, more than compensated for the discomforts of travel. We saw towering mountains. The Rockies are beautiful. There were great stretches of desert where it appears no one could ever live and then, after Cheyenne, Wyoming, onto the Great Plains.

Some of my fellow travelers thought me odd, but I love the plains most of all. They are as being on an ocean upon which one can walk. The sun slowly drifts down the curvature of the earth just as at sea, and the grasses, now gold and tall, break before the wind, blowing in great waves as do swells on the Pacific.

December 24, 1908. Christmas Eve. Our Lord's birthday is so different out here in the Wild West than on our ranch near Los Angeles. How I miss the wonderful cooking in Mexican style we had there.

The Medicine Lodge Cattle Company has invited all the neighboring ranchers and their families to spend Christmas Eve here in the big house. The children and I, along with the cook and some of the ranch hands, have been getting everything ready for the big celebration.

No one on the plains has electricity yet, even though there are rumors that it will be here someday. We have a huge Yuletide tree brought by the Union Pacific all the way from Wyoming. I'm told the tree was cut along the banks of the very creek that passes through our little valley. We are decorating the tree in the fashionable "White Tree" style. Our decorations will consist of cotton, tinsel, pinecones, icicles, and of course, plenty of candles, which the children are looking forward to lighting.

The children have been busy decorating. They even helped me set out luminarias today. I am trying to show them a custom from home and hope that it also helps a little, as I have grown homesick. We are all going to help prepare the great feast. We will have a host of wild turkeys Henry shot by the creek along with a slew of geese. Of course, we will also have great slabs of beef and potatoes. We are expecting a shipment of several cases of oysters packed in ice. The Union Pacific is supposed to bring them straight through from the east coast. Oh, how wonderful!

<u>December 25, 1908</u>. Christmas Day. Our party was a sight to behold. Over fifteen ranchers and their families came. We ate and ate. All the children opened presents that were gifts from my employers, Mr. and Mrs. Christie. The evening was truly memorable and the oysters were wonderful. After dinner, we danced the night away. Several of our cowboys are the most accomplished musicians. Violins, fiddles, guitars, and banjos; the music was wonderful.

I had the most wonderful dances with a rancher known as the Hero of the Table, or Cowboy George. They say he risked his own life fighting off a herd of rampaging longhorns to save his best friend who had been disemboweled by one of the beasts. George rescued the boy, but he died at home in his loving mother's arms. Anyway, in grateful recognition of his heroic acts, the rancher, Mr. Queen, and his wife gave the young hero enough range for his own ranch on the table.

Cowboy George is certainly the dapper young man. All the unmarried women are said to have set their caps for him. He asked me to dance so many times, Mrs. Queen told me he was absolutely smitten, and it looked as if I wouldn't be a teacher much longer. I assured her that was nonsense, he was just lonely and not many unwed females were at the party. She laughed and said I was much too pretty to go on being an old maid for much longer, and George had too much sense to let me get away. I was so embarrassed.

The most exciting news is that a ferocious blizzard hit after dinner last night and now, at noon on Christmas Day, it is still snowing and blowing terribly outside. You cannot even see your hand if you stick it out the door in the wind and snow. Of course, nobody went home. Everybody stayed here. The men stayed up most of the night drinking and playing cards and billiards, all of them except the young hero, George Roberts. After talking half the night away with me, he tied a long rope around his waist so he wouldn't get lost in the ferocious blizzard and went out to the barn to help the cowboys take care of everyone's animals. When he came back in for breakfast, he was covered with snow and his mustache was quite frozen. I asked him if he wasn't afraid of freezing his lungs. He laughed and asked me where I had ever heard such an old wife's tale. I assured him it was not and took my leave of such a rogue.

January 1, New Year's Day. 1909. There is a big dance tonight at the new Old Settlers Hall in Medicine Lodge. We are all going to the dance. We will be the envy of all; warm in furs and buffalo robes, riding to the dance in a sleigh pulled by two white horses with bells on their harness. People will come out of their houses just to see us go by.

I do wonder if Mr. Cowboy George Roberts will be there and if he will pay any attention to me or be lost among all the young women who hope to be a famous rancher's wife. Good for them. I have a fine relationship with my employers and could not hope for better.

January 2, 1909. We did not return to the ranch until well after midnight. The ride home was beautiful and romantic. The moon shone in the cloudless sky as if it were the world's most elegant pearl surrounded by thousands of diamonds. There was so much radiance we did not even need to light the lanterns.

We ladies snuggled deep into the robes and began to fall asleep just as warm and toasty as if we were all back in sunny California. We were quite happy slumbering away when the men started shooting their rifles and pistols at a wolf pack trailing along behind us. I even saw one of the brutes. Oh, he was an evil-looking beast, not at all resembling the dogs on the ranch. No wonder we lose so many cows to them. Guess who came riding up as fast as his horse could carry him through the snow? The heroic Cowboy George. He had one of the dreadful animals draped over the back of his saddle and said he was going to have it made into mittens and a cap for me. He was dashing on his fine horse, but as soon as he was gone I fell fast asleep again.

The dance was huge fun. I danced many times with George. All the other young women were quite beside themselves with envy. They tried their best to entice him, but he only had eyes for me. During the last dance, he was trying so hard to be a fine gentleman, he asked if he might come courting. I told him that would be fine if he continued to deport himself as a gentleman.

I suppose I should not have been surprised when he came galloping up to save us from those terrible wolves on the way home. Mrs. Queen was right. I do believe he is smitten.

March 28, 1909. Last night Mr. George Roberts, hero rancher of the North Table, formally asked for my hand in marriage. Since my own dear momma and papa passed away several years ago, George made his proposal through my employer and benefactor, Mr. Christie.

We have known each other such a short period of time that it is almost scandalous to consider such a proposal. Except, I have fallen deeply in love with dear George. I know he will be a fine husband and father. I told him I would consider this matter carefully, but I could not possibly marry him until he has started building us a fine home. I could not stand to live very long in the storm cellar he calls a house.

After discussing the matter with Mr. Christie, I relented, and we set the date for Sunday, June 13, 1909. By that time, he should be able to secure my replacement. The children have so much schooling left, little Jamie is learning his letters and Mattie is struggling with math.

I have so much to do. There are so many preparations to make I fear I will never get everything done.

Mr. and Mrs. Christie, bless them, announced they intend to hold the wedding here in the big house and invite all the cattlemen from the valley and the table. They said it would be the social event of the year. There will be a great feast and dancing. They also told me of a most curious custom on the plains. I should expect a *chivary*, where some of George's friends kidnap me on our very wedding night and hold me until my dear George meets their demands. They said he would have to do something silly like riding his horse backwards all the way around the pasture to win my freedom. They will also shoot off their guns, serenade us joyously, and play many other tricks.

<u>April 25, 1909</u>. Today, escorted by Mr. and Mrs. Christie, George took me riding to see our new house. It is right next to the storm cellar in which he has been

dwelling, and I fear I shall also for a while. He intends to make a doorway connecting the cellar to the basement so we have an escape in case of fire or danger.

Our house is close to an old buffalo wallow he loves. He has planted a cottonwood tree on its banks to symbolize our marriage. The house is wonderful. The downstairs will have a parlor, a dining room, a bedroom for us, and a huge kitchen. George has ordered a pump that goes inside the house so we can have freshwater directly in the kitchen. Upstairs there will be three bedrooms for our children. Both of us would like to have many. Soon, we hope, the house and the range will be noisy with the sound of little feet and the happy laughter of children.

George will teach the boys to be great ranchers, and I will show the girls how to be polite ladies. Of course, they will all do wonderful in their schooling, and all of them, even the girls, will go to college. I am convinced the only way to succeed in the future is through education.

I hear there is a new university in Boulder, Colorado, a town I should like to visit. It is so much closer than Lincoln, or maybe they shall go off to Laramie in Wyoming. Oh, how I shall miss them all!

June 15, 1909. What a wonderful time we have had at the new hotel on Lake Colton. George and I have had such walks and talks, and we have eaten so much. The hotel has such a wonderful bakery. We have had our fill of breads, cakes, and cookies.

Last night, the second night of our life together, George took me out to the garden, and we sat on benches under a glorious sky filled with stars. Dear George said he had something to say about his family he has always been afraid to tell me for fear I would never want to see him again. I told him he was just silly. Nothing he could ever say would make me not love him.

George's mother and father were outlaws in the Old West, and he was also until he ran off from them when he was only fourteen. He said his family was known as the Roberts Gang and other times as the Badlands Bunch. He has not heard from, nor seen them, since he left. He misses his father very much. He fears they are all dead, either killed in a shootout or as he puts it, "died from hanging around." George says his relatives have stretched rope in every town on the plains.

I told him he was daft. Of course, I do not love him any less for what his family was. Maybe I love him even a little more. I can just picture myself as part of the gang, riding around on fast horses and hiding out with my dear George.

<u>Thanksgiving Day. November 26, 1909</u>. We have been in our new house for almost a month. Last summer, George planted elm trees on the north and west sides of the house to protect us from the fierce winds. They will not stop very much wind or snow for a couple of years, but as we grow older, they will provide the shelter and shade we will require.

Our new pump has been delivered and George finished installing it last Monday. Thank heavens the weather has been perfect. It is nice and warm here on the plains instead of bitter and cold as it sometimes is at this time of the year. I expect bad weather soon. Great flocks of geese and ducks have been flying south and the hands say the wolves are running in their winter packs.

Our dinner consisted of goose, turkey, and beef. We had our three cowboys and our nearest neighbor, a recent immigrant by the name of Mr. Garl Schwartz to dinner.

117

George found him quite disagreeable and his views offensive on every subject. Dear George did not even serve whisky until after our guest had gone.

<u>December 7, 1909</u> Today, George finished the built-in closet in the north room upstairs and it is so beautiful. I will use it to store blankets while we wait for the babies to come. We are both ready for a family.

George gave me my Christmas present earlier today. He has purchased tickets for us on the Union Pacific. We are going to spend Christmas in Los Angeles. He has never seen the ocean, eaten an orange fresh off the tree, or even heard of avocados. We will have such fun!

Dear George will get to meet dear Consuelo and her younger brother Jesus, and he will discover how much I love and miss them. I pray that someday they might visit me on the plains and stay for a year. Would that not be wonderful?

<u>November 17, 1912</u>. George and I have now been married for over three years and have fallen comfortably into a life together running our little outfit and making it profitable. Both our horse and cattle herds are thriving. Of course, we continually have trouble getting them enough water. Fortunately, Mr. Christie allows us to drive them across his range to the creek in dry weather. The first two years we were married, there was enough water in the ponds and the wallow that we did not need to make the drive very often. This year has been terribly dry. Without Mr. Christie, all of our cows and horses would have positively dried up and blown away.

Last night, we could see the flames of a huge grass fire off to the north. Probably on Bull Horn Creek, George says. He has gone for a ride there today to see if he can lend a hand. He is such a nice man and always ready to help his neighbors. He says he has to make up for his outlaw years.

This has been a sad year for the world with the sinking of the Titanic. How our prayers go out to all the departed and their loved ones. It has also been a sad year for dear George and me. We lost our baby in August. I have not had the strength to write about it before. I had not been expecting very long. Mrs. Carrs, a woman who helps with birthing on the table, said she expected the weather was much too hot for a baby to come to a full birthing. Maybe that is true and our child was a victim of the drought; however, I am sometimes just so sad since then, that I must hide myself away and cry. Dear George tries to be encouraging, but life is hard on the table, and there is much work to be done on the ranch.

I do love our life on the prairie. I have learned to be quite a cowgirl, and I have taught George how to read and write and speak as a gentleman. He is now a member of the Cattlemen's Association and some say he is being groomed as the next president since his knows his letters. He is very proud that a former rustler and outlaw can rise so far in society. Our life would be perfect if only we had not lost our baby and if we could hear the sound of children playing. I am lonely for them.

Last night, Dear George told me one more bit of news about his past, which he said he could no longer keep secret from me. In 1906, just after he became a rancher and was still quite young, he was hanging around a saloon in Ogallala when a gunfighter from Colorado came up to him at the bar and said he was looking for this "big hero Cowboy George" everybody was always taking about. He told George he had even heard of him in a bar in Leadville, a Colorado mining town high in the mountains and came all this way to prove that he was a bigger hero than some flatlander in Nebraska.

George said he did a terrible thing, but he had been drinking and maybe he had not been thinking too clearly. Anyway, George told the gunfighter who he was and the man said he reckoned he knew that anyway. Well, the gunman from the mountains started backing up, and everyone in the bar but my poor George started jumping for a place to hide. George said that as soon as they stopped backing-up, he figured the man would try to take his pistol from his holster in a quick manner and shoot him dead. That my dear husband is still alive, he assured me, is a testimony to God's holy protection and years of practice with guns. He learned the skills of firearms from his father. Life on the run taught him many skills for survival. Learning the fast draw from his father saved his life.

Sometimes I think my George has led such a terribly exciting and dangerous life that he must find me quite boring, especially since I am so sad much of the time. But, he says he loves me more than ever and would not be able to live without me.

February 20, 1913. I am excited and so happy. I just told George that we should expect our baby to be born in September. I missed my monthlies twice in a row and became ill as I fried his morning steak and eggs yesterday and today. Finally, we are going to start our family! This baby will stay in me until he is ready to come out and be quite the little cowboy.

We danced around and around the house. We are so happy. This is the happiest I have felt since I was expecting our first child. I just know everything will be fine from now on, and I will be the happiest woman on the table.

<u>May 10, 1913</u>. George and the hands are out on the range searching for lost cattle after the terrible blizzard of last week. He thinks our losses are high, but we will be just fine. He is doing everything he can, but this winter has been too cold, windy, and dreary. We never see the sun, and it has snowed almost every day. The wind has not stopped blowing since last fall. Sometimes I think I will go to the basement and curl up in a ball if the wind does not stop soon.

This should be the happiest time of my life, but I am sad and feel as if I am growing sadder each day. I long for the ocean and the warm sun. I would love to smell green grass and ripening fruit. Nothing green, gentle, or warm can be found here on the prairie. I feel all alone. I could just die, but for the baby.

Oh, how I miss Consuelo and the wonderful dinners her mama would make. I miss the sounds of the Mexican language and the colorful clothing. Most of the women I see when we go into the Medicine Lodge mercantile for supplies are the wives of immigrants and new farmers. They are fencing off our beloved open range, plowing under the grass, and trying to grow crops. The women are all stout and red-faced; they work as hard in the fields as the men and none of them speaks English. Oh, I hope George never wants me to clean out his barns with a pitchfork. If I get any sadder or lonelier, I will just sit down and cry without stopping.

<u>August 13, 1913</u>. I have grown extremely large, and the heat is wilting every plant, even the rhubarb, which is such a sturdy vegetable. Many days, I just take to my bed and lie there crying and crying. I want to stop, I want to

jump out of bed and be the wife George deserves, but I cannot. I fear I never will be again.

It has been months since I cooked or cleaned or fulfilled any of my other wifely duties. I tell myself to get up and be happy, that our baby will make everything wonderful again, and the poor little thing will need a happy mother so he or she can grow up straight and tall. I do not know how I shall ever get up out of this bed.

The heat is so cruel, and everything on this horrible prairie is so ugly. It is all brown, and the dust from the fields of turned sod is constantly blowing. Just yesterday I attempted to sit in the shade of the house, but the blowing dust and the hot wind conspired to drive me back inside. On the way to the front door, I almost stepped on the biggest rattlesnake I have ever seen. I killed it with the hoe George brought me so I could try to cultivate enough land to grow some lilacs.

August 14, 1913. Today I have wonderful news. George telegraphed Mr. and Mrs. Briggs, and they have agreed to allow Consuelo to come and stay with us. She will help care for the baby and be a great friend to me. Jesus must come along also. That will be great fun, but I am surprised such a pleasant boy would be eager to leave all his friends in sunny California and come here. He never seemed the type who would like to ride horses, herd cattle, and do all the other hard work required on the range. I am glad they are coming. They will arrive at the depot in one week.

I am excited and have much to do to make us ready for their arrival. I shall have Consuelo stay in the north room. She can use George's beautiful built-in closet. Jesus will stay in the east room, and when the baby is old enough to move upstairs, the warm south room will be just the place.

Our house is about to come alive with joy. We shall have our baby and our friends. Dear George has showed again why he is the nicest man in the world. I am so happy. The weather is cooling today, and we have had the nicest rain. Everything outside is drenched, the air smells fresh and the dirt has stopped blowing.

<u>September 1, 1913</u>. Consuelo and Jesus arrived this afternoon on the three o'clock train. We hugged and hugged until George finally made us get back into the wagon and leave for the ranch. I know I should not have taken such a long ride in my condition, but dear George made me a soft bed in the back. I hardly felt a jolt as he is such a considerate driver, and our road is in such fine condition.

Consuelo is so beautiful, and as soon as we arrived at the ranch, she insisted on making us one of her mama's finest dinners. She even brought a box full of chilies with her. Even George, who claims not to be partial to Mexican-style cooking, had to admit the meal was wonderful.

I am concerned about Jesus, though Consuelo assures me he will be fine. He seems much too delicate to work outside with the men. He looks just like Consuelo with his beautiful hair and long eyelashes. I discussed this with George, and he told me that if Jesus wishes to stay and work in the house with the ladies, that would be just fine. He has no use outside for a hand who cannot pull his own weight.

It is settled then. If Jesus wishes to work in and around the house, that will be fine. Consuelo says he is a bright boy. He is a poet and has somewhat of a following in Los Angeles for his pen. I intend to listen to him recite soon.

<u>September 5, 1913</u>. This morning I was delivered of a beautiful baby boy. Mrs. Carrs did not make it in time. She was clear north on the Platte helping deliver twins. Consuelo, however, said she had birthing experience and took over, sending poor nervous George out to the barn. Consuelo and Jesus were wonderful and knew just what to do. What would I ever have done without them?

We will call the little one Donald after my grandfather. This Donald Roberts shall grow up to be a great man, maybe he will even be president of these very United States.

<u>October 30, 1913</u>. Not only is George Roberts the proud father of the most beautiful little boy in the whole world, but he is now President of the Western Nebraska Cattleman's Association. He is getting to be an important man.

We are all happy together. Consuelo and Jesus are delighted to be here on the prairies and in the cool weather. Whenever it is warm enough, we wrap little Donald in his blankets and go on long rides. Yesterday, we found a vast field of buffalo bones and came upon a small number of Indians who had come all the way down from their reservation in South Dakota to pray. They were very nice and shared a little of their food with us. I do hope I did not eat some poor puppy.

The chief, a most handsome man and the leader of a beauteous people, spoke halting English. He explained that one of the last of the great buffalo herds was killed there. To them, it is a very sacred place. If they pray hard enough, they believe the buffalo will come back and roam the earth again.

The man was carrying a rifle, just like the one George has hanging over the mantle as a souvenir of his days on the run. George calls it a Yellow Boy because of the beautiful brass. The old chief smiled when he told me it was his medicine gun he used in the big fight against Long Hair Custer on the Little Big Horn. I wished George would have been along. He and the old man probably would have talked about the Old West for most of the day. When we told George and he rode off this morning to find them, he only came upon a smoldering fire. They have all gone back to their own lands.

January 10, 1914. We have been snowed-in now for nearly a week. The weather stayed beautiful and warm until the day after Christmas, but it has not stopped snowing since. George and the cowboys have been able to clear off the stock tanks and keep the cows watered. Thankfully he was able to store enough hay last summer to keep them fed through the time when the snow is so deep.

I do worry about Jesus. His poetry is beautiful and he continues to write, but he is becoming more like a woman than a man. Yesterday, I even found him in his room dressed in Consuelo's clothing. He looked just like her. I thought it was her and began talking, until he turned around and smiled at me. I was so embarrassed, I ran back downstairs.

I fear the prairies are too rough for a boy of his nature. George admitted he is worried also. He tried to be delicate, but I found it upsetting when he told me that girl-boys, a strange name, are treated badly around here. He would not tell me what happens to them, considering it too indelicate for my ears.

<u>May 5, 1914</u>. Yesterday was a real surprise for both of us. George's family has come to live on our ranch. He thought they were all dead, but his mother, Uncle Roy and Aunt Rosie, their two small children, and George's little brother, Autie, traveled all the way from the badlands of South Dakota in an old wagon. George barely remembers Autie, who is a lot younger than he is, but Autie can already read and write and he hero-worships his big brother.

George is very happy to get to know his little brother, but was quite distressed to learn his father was hanged in Wyoming four years ago. Autie was with him at the time. It must have been an awful tribulation for a boy to be forced to watch his father die. Autie rode alone all the way from Yellowstone to the Badlands of South Dakota to find his mother, stopping only long enough to burn down a barn on the ranch where the cowboys who had killed his father worked. He read in the papers about George being elected president of the Cattlemen, and here they are.

I am trying very hard to be a lady, as is Consuelo, around George's mother, but it is difficult. She is an unwashed woman and very bossy, often referring to Consuelo and Jesus as "greasers." She seems to delight in making poor Jesus miserable, calling him a "Mexican girl," or a "señorita." Just this morning I even heard her call him a "dirty little queer," but I will never tell George.

We moved George's mother - I cannot bring myself to call her Molly - into the north room where Consuelo had been sleeping after she insisted that would be her place. Consuelo is now sharing the east room with Jesus and both of them say it is a wonderful arrangement. Nevertheless, I made George hang several sheets across the middle of the room so they may have some privacy.

George's aunt and uncle are fixing an apartment in the barn and Autie has moved into the bunkhouse as a full-fledged cowboy.

<u>March 16, 1917</u>. George made me swear to secrecy this morning, and then he told me his worst fears. He believes his mother, aunt and uncle, and even Autie have returned to their outlaw ways. He suspects they are using our home as a safe haven and are stealing cattle and horses on their long absences.

They led George to believe they were searching for land for their own place, but too many odd circumstances have come to his attention. All of his relatives suddenly have new horses, fancy new clothes, and new weapons. He promised he would send them all away, even his mother and Autie, if it is true they are riding the outlaw trail.

I dare not tell him that his mother, Uncle Roy, and Aunt Rosie are quite open around Consuelo and Jesus. They demand to be waited on hand and foot, ordering them around as if they are servants, and talking about their stealing. Consuelo came to me afraid and asked what she should do. I told her she must never say anything to George or anyone else. I was sure he would find out on his own.

<u>April 20, 1917</u>. A terrible thing has happened. Today in town, George read a wanted poster about a gang of rustlers operating along the Platte. The poster had a description of the thieves and the horses and weapons they had taken along with fifty head of cattle. Poor George knew the thieves were was his mother, Uncle Roy, Aunt Rosie, and Autie. Under his questioning, they admitted to their wrongdoing and even tried to get him to join them.

Alan Hafer

He gave them until tonight to leave or he will turn them over to the local sheriff. I shall miss Autie very much. Nevertheless, I finally had to confess to George that his relatives often talked about their robberies in the parlor. We will all be much happier without them, but I feel sorry for George. He found his lost family, only to send them away. I would never tell dear George, but his mama is not a nice person. It is small wonder he remembers his father so fondly and has little to say about her.

I thought Consuelo and Jesus would be quite pleased to see them go since they were so mean. Maybe they just miss Autie who is their age, but they have locked themselves in their room since I told them George's family was leaving. I can hear crying in there, but when I ask if I can help, Consuelo always says it is nothing. I do hope they are all right.

Donald is growing quite big for his age of four. He makes us laugh every day with his playing. He has his own pony and is quite the little cowboy. Our life on the prairie is full of hard work, much happiness, and some sadness.

I fear that we shall never have another child. Even if we do not, Donald brings enough happiness and joy into our lives. We are blessed to have him, as we are to have Consuelo and Jesus.

June 4, 1918. We begin every morning with a prayer for our boys fighting in the awful European war. Several of the brave men from the table are in France. I say an extra little prayer for them and their poor families every night.

George's mother, aunt, and uncle are back in Medicine Lodge. They purchased some small acreage close to the creek and claim that they are going to grow vegetables. Dear George believes they must have stolen enough money to support themselves for a while, but he

128

doubts they will ever leave the outlaw trail. Most likely, he says they will stretch hemp someday in Medicine Lodge. He will be embarrassed when he has to explain the mother of the President of the Cattleman's Association is a cattle thief.

George attempted to pay his relatives a visit. He was going to plead with them not to go back to stealing, but they would not speak to him. His uncle became angry and ordered him off his property while pointing a rifle at him. His mother screamed out the window that Autie was her only son.

Autie is working for the Bull Horn Creek Land and Cattle Company. He lives in a line shack only about ten miles from here. For some reason, Jesus and Consuelo became quite fearful hearing he was so close. I do not know what happened between them, but it must have been serious.

<u>March 3, 1919</u>. George's Uncle Roy and Aunt Rosie purchased more land and now have one of the largest farms south of Medicine Lodge. George says he expects they will escape the noose now that they have become such large landowners. His mother, Molly, spends most of her time in the saloon. Every night some equally drunk man takes her home or she sleeps behind the barbershop, waiting to start drinking in the morning again.

George has offered to help his mother, but she will not talk to him. Autie is still supposed to be with Bull Horn Creek. George heard in town he has become a foreman, but he will not speak to either George or me. Rumor has it Autie offered to take Molly to the ranch with him so she could live as a good and decent woman. She told him that she would much rather be a drunk in Medicine Lodge than to have anything to do with the modern times. We are told that when she is drunk she cries for George's father and the outlaw ways. She says she wishes she could just die rather than live any longer when her kind no longer exists.

January 7, 1920. Old Schwartz, the only man on the table George does not hold as a friend, has returned from Denver. He went there to learn about an organization called the Ku Klux Klan.

The secret organization began as a gathering of white southerners who joined together to protect white women from the supposed rampaging lust of black men. I do not hold at all with their ways. They now profess to hate Catholics, Hebrews, immigrants, and anyone who speaks a foreign language as much as they do the Negro. I cannot understand why they would let Schwartz into their group since he is a German immigrant. I guess he convinced them he is a good American.

The members, or Klanners as George calls them, wear white robes and masks with eyeholes cut out so they can see. They seem to be fond of burning crosses when they meet. George is going to attend their meeting tonight in the new Methodist Church. I surely do not know why; he professes to hate no man or race, save perhaps Old Schwartz. He did learn that after they adjourned, the Klan would be buying whiskey for everyone who attends. George says it will be quite humorous to drink with men who claim to be opposed to alcohol. I reminded him we need him at home, and he should not spend too long drinking with hate-filled men.

June 21, 1920. That awful man, Old Schwartz, is the leader of the local Klan, and the members, though some have been friends of George's in the past, are quite as hate-filled as their leader. We have heard they have discussed Consuelo and Jesus at their meetings, even going so far as to say George and I harbor traitorous papists, greaser Mexicans, and abominations to God.

Consuelo and Jesus are like our own family. They are Americans, not Mexicans, and in this country, we are free to worship as we choose. I surely do not know of what they speak when they call them abominations. I am most confused because George's Uncle Roy does most of the shouting against Consuelo and Jesus. Perhaps he is such a mean man he wishes to hurt us through them.

George has also heard that Autie hangs around the group but does not have much to say. George has not returned to their meetings since the first one he attended. He always says that no whiskey in the county is strong enough to make him forget the ugliness he saw there.

<u>July 1, 1920</u>. Yesterday, while we were in town, someone left a note on our wagon saying the Klan is coming to our house tonight. The note said they are going to send Jesus and Consuelo back to California. George says not to worry; he will not allow such a terrible thing to happen.

I pray that with God's help and George's skill with weapons we shall all be safe from harm. Dear George has sent little Donald, Jesus, Consuelo and me to the storm shelter where I am writing this entry. He told the ranch hands that this was not their fight and sent them away, even though they all protested and said they would back him in any fight with a bunch of fool farmers. George is now sitting out in front in his rocker with his new rifle across his lap. His beloved yellow boy is propped within reach against the porch.

I know dear George will protect us. God will not allow any harm to come to Donald or our beloved Jesus and Consuelo. We are going to sing songs and play games during our confinement.

I have lit the lanterns so we can see. George says that a storm and the Klan are on the way. He can hear them both. He told me to turn out the lantern, but Jesus is very afraid.

May God protect us in this day of our need.

July 5, 1920. This will be the last entry I ever make. I hope I am strong enough to write this down. Jesus and Consuelo were horribly murdered in the storm cellar while the Klan was here. Little Donald is fine, I do not know if he saw anything or not. Dear God, please help him forget what he saw that day.

My husband George believes I did it. I do not know. I do not remember anything. We were singing songs and then the Klan came. I do not remember anything else until George was washing the blood from my poor murdered darlings off my face. I do not know how I could have done such a terrible act. George says nobody else could have. He believes I blacked out under the strain, having another attack of the melancholies as he puts it, and killed them. Oh God. They are dead and at peace, but I shall have to suffer the rest of my life.

George is burying poor Jesus and Consuelo in the cellar and covering their grave with steel so they will never be found. He said we shall not speak of their murders again. We shall tell everyone they ran from the Klan and must have made their way back to California.

I am now going to bury my journals with my darlings. I cannot imagine who would want to read about the life of a murderess.

CHAPTER FIFTEEN

IT WAS MIDNIGHT AND THE GRANDFATHER CLOCK IN THE parlor didn't strike twelve; it hadn't struck anything since nine o'clock in the morning, March 6, 1957. The date and time held no real significance - it was the day the clock stopped. Adam's family had never been able to start it again. Because the clock reminded them of Grandma Sarah, his parents had left it in the corner.

Adam had just finished the last of Sarah's journals and placed the brittle volume on the table with the others. His mind wasn't just swimming with new information, it was drowning. He was angry there was so much he hadn't known and so much about his family that no one had spoken of.

Why did they keep this from him? Did they keep it from his father? Had he forgotten what happened in the cellar? Had his mom and dad been part of a conspiracy? How else could you explain the silence? Had his Grandmother Roberts, remembered by most as a sickly woman when she died in the late 1940's, been a crazed murderess? Was she the crazy old woman of his dreams?

No wonder his family had been so split. He'd always doubted the truth in the axiom 'thick as thieves'. Now he'd learned his own family was proof that a life of crime did not make for strong family ties.

Did the cousins he and his brother fought with years ago know any of this? What about his poor grandmother? She wrote only once in her journal after the murders, living the rest of her life with the person she loved most believing she was insane and had killed her best friends. As a child, he had always thought her to be a moody, anxious woman. No wonder she had died young.

Adam supposed his father hadn't remembered that night. He had probably repressed it from his memory as a child but had lived with it prodding his conscious. He'd always thought, as did his mother, that his father's anger and anxiety were genetic, an inheritance from Sarah - a gift Adam had also received. Now he wondered if their primary problem started that dark night in the storm cellar.

If Adam's ghosts were merely dreams, maybe his father, in a somnambulist moment, had recalled the murders when he was asleep on one of those long nights he'd pulled the duty of feeding his second son a bottle. Perhaps Adam had heard him talking in his sleep, incorporated the story into his memory banks, and had suffered every since. Maybe his father, known only to his subconscious, knew his mother hadn't committed the murders and told Adam who then dreamed of her proclaiming her innocence.

Historians would want to study the journals. Anthropologists and state authorities would demand to examine the bodies. Cynthia would surely want the Medicine Lodge Museum of History to display the volumes, probably a portion of the steel tomb cover, and the artifacts from the cellar.

As soon as this all became public, a history of the Roberts family would hit the bookstores. Adam could just imagine the title: *The Badlands Bunch: The Roberts Family of Outlaws*. Or, *The Roberts Family: Horse Thieves and Knife Murderers*. Maybe even, *Sarah Roberts: The First Dahmer*.

Would Nebraska make a celebration out of trying Sarah Roberts for the murders of Jesus and Consuelo Vargas in 1920? Adam remembered a similar case that had taken place in Cheyenne, Wyoming. They had retried the famous regulator Tom Horn for the murder of little Willie Nickells in 1903. Colorado recently held a retrial for Alfie Packer, an infamous miner charged with cannibalism in 1874, and accused by the judge of eating three of the only four Republicans in Hinsdale County.

Adam could even imagine Klan members making secret visits to the property. He could come to only one conclusion. He didn't believe Sarah, George, Donald Roberts, or Consuelo and Jesus Vargas deserved such a fate. They were all gone now. Let them rest in peace.

He opened the refrigerator, took out a frost-covered can of beer, and sat on the front steps. The wind blowing out of the west was cool; if it had been one month later, he would have thought it a harbinger of an early fall. It wasn't the temperature, but he couldn't escape the feeling that something was wrong. The world wasn't as it should have been. Something in the universe was out of balance.

"That's it! The moon is coming up too far north. It's too yellow and too low for this time of night," he yelled, jumping to his feet. "Oh shit!! That's not the moon, it's a fire. It's close to the farm!" he screamed at the top of his voice.

Adam ran across the yard and saw the source of the fire was the old cottonwood marking the graves. Engulfed in flames, the old symbol of Cowboy George's love for Sarah was slowly toppling over onto the burial plot of the two young Hispanics who'd traveled from California to help raise their son.

Adam ran to save the small white cross he'd erected, but the fire was so hot he couldn't get close. Throwing up his hands to shelter his face from the heat, he was defenseless. He never knew anyone was behind him. Stars caused by the blow to the back of his head exploded even brighter than the fire, but only for a microsecond. He was unconscious before he started falling.

Adam was climbing, sometimes swirling on strong currents of pain, back to consciousness. Slowly, he became aware of sharp gravel poking into the left side of his face. A large grasshopper perched above his right eye. Even though the pain in the back of his head was intense, feeling the insect's movement was disgusting. Swatting it away brought more pain, and he wondered if it had been worth the effort.

He had no idea how long he had been unconscious. He wondered about the time, but he'd left his watch in the house. He couldn't sit up without pain and decided to spend the rest of the night where he was.

Adam knew better than to sleep with a head injury, but if he was going to die he would rather go in his sleep than staying awake and worrying about it. He also hoped whoever attacked him was long gone.

The sun peering over the horizon, its rays bouncing off a steel granary and directly into his eyes, awakened him a few hours later. He had still a horrible headache and felt like vomiting, but he could walk. However, he stopped and stared in disbelief when he saw his car. Totally demolished, the eight-year-old RX-11, his pride and joy, would never again leave the yard under its own power. Cars had passed through crushers, baled, and emerged in better condition.

He stumbled to the house, barely able to read the words, "Get Out Or Get Dead" painted in red on the white wood of the door. Clearly, his attackers were men of few words.

Adam needed help and a friend. Cynthia said she'd be out within fifteen minutes. He was lying on the bed when she brought him ice water and aspirin. When she saw his car, she became angry. When she ran behind the granaries and saw the cottonwood, she went ballistic.

The quiet museum coordinator was swearing when she ran back inside the house and grabbed the phone, attacking the rotary model Adam's brother had left in the house with such anger he was afraid she was going to tear off the dial. Dialing and then tapping her foot on the floor while waiting for an answer on the other end, she looked at him, trying her best to smile through the tears welling up in her eyes.

"Hello. Who is this?" she demanded, running her fingers through the brown hair she had confessed to Adam was salt and pepper when not dyed.

"Well, Chief Clark," she said after the person on the other end of the line introduced himself, "I thought fire departments fought fires. Are you guys on strike or something?"

Another pause. "Well then, how come nobody came out to the old Roberts place last night and put out the fire that burned the most famous cottonwood tree on the table to charcoal? The flames must have been so bright you could see them from town. Surely somebody reported it to you."

"Uh-huh. Now let me get this straight." Clearly taken by surprise, Cynthia was staring at Adam as if he might turn out to be the murderer. "Somebody called the station a little after midnight last night, identified himself as

Adam Roberts, and told you not to worry about the fire. He said his family had decided the tree was rotten and dangerous and asked him to burn it down. In fact, he said several of his brothers and their families were out there having a wake for the old tree."

Her expression changed from anger to disbelief as she listened for a moment. "Oh. I see. You thought they must have been having one hell of a party burning down the old tree because the person who called you sounded like a drunk."

Again listening intently, tapping her fingers on the destroyed kitchen counter, she paused before she spoke. "Well. I guess you'd better come out here and talk with Adam Roberts himself," a caustic smile played across her face as she winked at him. "He says he doesn't know anything about a wake or a family decision. He says he ran out to see what was burning and somebody knocked him unconscious."

Adam assumed the fire chief must have questioned whether he was telling the truth. "Well, darn, Chief, you know he could be lying," she said. "But he's here on a couch, blood on his face and matted in his hair with a huge bump on the back of his head. If he wasn't unconscious, he's one damn great actor."

This time she listened only for a second and must have interrupted the chief. "Uh. I'll let you know about that. He'll call the sheriff if he wants to file a complaint. Bye now."

After hanging up the phone, she turned and stared at Adam with a look that was not one of lust. "And now, my fine gentleman," she ordered while placing an ice pack on his forehead, "You need to call the sheriff - or I will. You should have filed a complaint when someone shot at you, except the only explanation you could think of was that weak, female little me had spilled the beans to her husband about your sexual peccadilloes. Adam, think about it. Someone is out to hurt you, and it's not my husband. He's fishing a thousand miles away from here. You have to report this."

At least she was half-right. He had thought she'd told her husband and blamed the affair on him, claiming he had swept her off her feet with his big city ways and used her for his own savage needs. He had a lot to learn about sixty-year-olds having affairs, but this was not the time for a lesson.

"Cynthia, I apologize for thinking your husband did this. I was wrong to have doubted you, but I was right not to involve the police."

"Oh yeah. You were right. You were so right you almost died last night. I don't know who is doing this, but so far they've shot at you, they've knocked you out, and the most historic tree around Medicine Lodge has burned to the ground. What's next? Some morning I go to the museum and find your body drained of blood and hanging upside down from the front door?"

"Now that might be a little over the top, I don't think a vampire is stalking me." He said with a weak smile.

"Listen, Adam. I want you in my life. As a friend. Maybe as a friend with privileges, but, I want you alive. You have a family in Colorado that loves you. Think about them. We would all feel terrible if you died. But I won't go to your funeral. I don't want to have a good cry over your coffin next to your wife and kids."

"Cynthia, do you mean it when you say you're concerned about my wife? I mean, you're my lover. How can you be sympathetic to my wife?"

"Look. This isn't about your dick," Cynthia retorted, her face hardening with anger. "It's about your life. Of course, I'm concerned about your family. What on earth do you think I am? A twenty-year-old bimbo who wants to destroy your family and marry you for your money? You are my friend, and I'm worried about you. If you don't get it together quick, you won't be such a good friend in the future."

"I'm sorry. You're right. And I do have a lot to learn about real friendships, I expect. But I can't report this to the police. Not yet. Maybe never."

"Then I'm going back to work," she said over her shoulder as she walked to the door. "Don't call me again. I don't want to be the one who finds you dead. Your wife and kids need to hold your bleeding, dying ass. Not me."

She was almost out of the house before he was able to grab her shoulder and turn her around. "Don't you see," he pleaded, trying to gather a thousand thoughts into one coherent argument. "Whoever is doing this killed Jesus and Consuelo Vargas or knows who did. For some reason, fear of discovery has made the killer paranoid. It's as if the past eighty years have deepened the hatred that caused two murders.

"Obviously, someone much younger is helping him. I mean, a one-hundred-year-old guy would have trouble burning up a tree and then running over to the shed to knock me out. Call me a chauvinist, but I can't imagine it being a woman. It has to be a man, and I would expect someone that old to have little bottles of laxative instead of light beer littering the ground where he waited to shoot at me.

"Besides, think about this. If they wanted me dead, I would be. Whoever it is had a perfect opportunity last night. He could have killed me, thrown my body on the fire, and made sure burning branches fell on me. The sheriff would have called it a freak of nature, at least an act of God, and the killers would have been home free.

"Someone is trying to frighten me. Someone who was alive in 1920. And that should reduce our suspect population to a controllable number. Help me find out who it is. Then we'll find out who killed Jesus and Consuelo and why this tragedy happened."

Once again, she turned to leave and spoke over her shoulder on the way out. "You need to stay alive more than you need to find out why somebody killed two people eighty years ago. Even if we call the police, we can still research the past. Report it, and we'll go back to work."

"Cynthia, it's not about me," he said, enveloping her in as much of a hug as his headache would allow. "Can't you see that? It's about my parents and grandparents. It's about their privacy, and it's about the dignity of the murdered kids. Don't they all deserve the chance to rest in peace? Besides, what about you and your museum? You may have the Nebraska historical find of the last fifty years."

"Leave me and the museum out of this," she interrupted. "I won't be the cause of your death. But what do you mean about your parents and grandparents."

"Okay. Look. I didn't call you last night because I was reading my grandmother's journals I found in the tomb. . . ."

"Your grandmother's journals? You found them? Did you know she kept any? No, of course you didn't. Nobody did, did they? But they must have buried them in 1920? Oh, my God!" The curator part of her personality was kicking into high gear. Adam had her complete attention.

"That's what I figure," he said, handing the volumes to her. "She started writing when she was still in California and had just learned she got a job as tutor for the kids on the Medicine Lodge Cattle Company. She called it, *Life and Times on the Plains.* These books are a record of her life from 1908 to 1920.

"I read about my grandpa being a hero and a gunfighter who killed a man in a shootout. Consuelo and Jesus Vargas came to live with them because Grandma began displaying symptoms of depression while she was pregnant. My grandfather made her, my father, and Jesus and Consuelo go down into the storm cellar while he waited for the Klan with his rifle."

Cynthia's excitement about the old journals transcended her fears. Opening one of the books, she began reading. "My God. That's all in here? What else? Oh, this is wonderful! Right here are her recipes for their 1911 Christmas dinner."

She was so absorbed in his grandmother's records that Adam couldn't get her attention. Finally, he had to reach out and lower the book from her eyes. "There's a lot more. My father's grandparents were outlaws, known as the Roberts Gang or the Badlands Bunch. My grandfather ran away from them to go straight when he was fourteen. That's how he ended up working on the ranch and rescued the boy from the longhorn. My great-grandfather stretched rope as a horse thief in Wyoming while his youngest son, a great-uncle I never knew existed, watched. It seems as if my great-grandmother, Molly, was a hardcore crook and never gave up her outlaw ways, even after she came to live with my grandparents.

"And one other point. Something bad happened between Autie, my grandfather's younger brother, and Jesus and Consuelo. Something so bad they were afraid of him. What happened, what caused their fear, may be the answer. That's what we need to find out."

"Adam, I, Uh. Can the museum have these?" Cynthia asked, now as caught up in the historical importance of the journals as he knew she would be. "You can keep ownership, but we'll put them on display. I even know who to call at the university. We'll have them published. You and your family will be famous."

"I know, and that's what my brothers and I have to talk about before any of this becomes public. We have a lot to consider. We need to make some decisions. Do we want our story told? My grandfather tried so hard to hide his past, do we betray him if we make it public? What if my grandmother was an insane killer? After all, she was alone in the cellar with my father and the two murdered kids. Her last entry says my grandfather thought she did it. He was trying to protect her when he hid the bodies. Does my family want our grandmother known as the Lizzy Borden of the Plains?

"Cynthia, I can't decide this alone. I need to speak with my brothers. And we need to talk to our kids. Surely you understand?"

"Of course I do, when you put it that way," she whispered, hugging him with sympathy and understanding. "Let's do this. You go and check into the motel, clean up, find something to eat, and rest. Call your wife and kids. I'm sure they are just sick with worry.

"If you'll trust me, I'm going to leave immediately for Lincoln and get on the state's computers and search all of their records. If anyone from Medicine Lodge in 1920 who was old enough to have been with the Klan then is still alive, I'll find him. I'm also going to do a trace on Autie. We need to know what happened to him. Maybe we can find someone still alive he told his story to."

CHAPTER SIXTEEN

ADAM WAS HALFWAY TO SIDNEY BEFORE HE REMEMBERED head injury victims shouldn't drive. Awakened by the blaring lights and air horn of an eighteen-wheeler, he barely avoided a collision by steering his brother's vintage pickup off the side of the highway and down a steep embankment towards the railroad tracks.

Wrenching hard on the wheel, only the left tires staying in contact with the ground, the Korean War-era pickup turned away from the freight train speeding towards him. However, he now headed toward a lot holding tons of beef for the Omaha markets.

Manure thrown over the fence every day for the past twenty years and compacted by the elements into soft mounds threw the old truck back towards the highway. Stopping after he was back on the paved shoulder of the Interstate to catch his breath, he felt as if someone had hit him over the head again. If nothing else, Adam had scared himself into another terrible headache.

He drove slowly the rest of the way to the motel. After begging a first floor room because he didn't have the energy to climb steps or push the buttons on an elevator, Adam sprawled out on the bed, asleep within five minutes of registering.

He slept until the telephone awakened him sixteen hours later. His headache was now a dull throb. At least it didn't feel as if his brains were on fire any longer. "Hello," was all he could think of to say. If the person on the other end of the line didn't know who he was, they were both in trouble. Adam wasn't sure who he was either.

"Well hello yourself," Cynthia replied. "Gee! You sound chipper this morning. I'll bet you didn't go to the doctor, did you? For all I knew, you were lying there dead. I worried you wouldn't even make it to the motel. I don't know what I was thinking when I let you drive."

"Hello Cynthia. Where are you? Last I remember you were going to drive to Lincoln."

"That was at three o'clock yesterday afternoon. I got here late last night, and I've spent the last two hours in the library. Wait until you hear what I found out. I just wanted to know you were all right before I started back. You're going to be so excited."

"Good. That's wonderful. What's thrilling? Are you going to tell me or do I have to guess?"

"Of course I'm going to tell you." Cynthia spoke with an inflection in her voice that made it sound as though she thought his head injury had given him brain damage. "I'll tell you the whole story as soon as I get there, but for right now think about this. Autie is alive. Your great-uncle Autie who knew Consuelo and Jesus, who scared them, is still alive. We'll go see him as soon as I get back."

Suddenly learning so much about his family after sixty years of knowing nothing was adding up to a case of cognitive overload. Adam was able to mumble only, "Give me a minute will you," after she breathlessly asked what he thought. He had to get over the shock. When he finally spoke, for reasons he couldn't explain, he felt a great sense of loss. "Okay. I'm ready now. Where is he? Where's he been all this time? What else was did my family keep from me?"

"Adam, I don't know what all your folks didn't tell you, but Autie lives in a rest home in Oklahoma. He's not there now. I'll tell you about it. I'll be at your hotel before eight o'clock tonight. Go back to sleep and then get something to eat. See you in a while!"

Slowly the 'oh-poor-me' syndrome he was experiencing gave way to excitement. His great-uncle, the man who might have killed Jesus and Consuelo, who certainly had known them, was still alive. He was the only person who could unravel the mystery and answer all his other questions about the Roberts family

Adam was too excited to go back to sleep. He had to talk to his brothers. It was time for them to act as a family. With any luck, he could get two of the three together that afternoon, and they could find a way to get the other one on the phone.

Adam called his older sibling, Jake, and told him he had the most important family news of his life. He asked him to call their younger brother, Ben, who lived in the Sand Hills, to meet them at the farmhouse at two that afternoon and to bring a speakerphone so they could talk to their youngest brother, Joe, in Texas. He set the meeting at the old house because it was the only place to discuss such information. That was where it had all happened. His brothers could see for themselves the tomb where their grandfather had buried Jesus and Consuelo.

Adam had forgotten about the damage to the old place, including the fire-destroyed tree. As he drove up in the sputtering pickup, the last one to his own meeting, his brothers rushed out into the yard. From the looks on their faces, they were madder than he'd seen them in years.

"What in the hell is going on out here, for Christ's sake," his older brother, Jake, yelled. "Why is your car a wreck, and why are you driving my old truck? Hell's fire! I only drive that old junker down to the corner once in a while to make sure it still runs."

"The tree," his younger brother, Ben, called out as livid as their older sibling. "That old cottonwood has been there for almost one hundred years. We built swings in its branches and played on it when we were kids. You've been here for less than a week, and you've burned it down!"

"Not to mention the house." Jake turned around and pointed at their childhood home. "Our house is a wreck! It's uninhabitable! You've torn it up. It looks like you shot out an upstairs window. You even dug up the lilacs and rhubarb. I was going to tend them starting this fall. Now it's a mess and there's steel in the ground. Jesus! You could screw up a junk yard."

Adam remembered them as always being excitable and had thought it a condition associated with living in unpopulated areas. They never had anything important to worry about, so they overreacted. On second thought, he supposed this wasn't so little, and this was not the time to tease them about being residents of a bucolic setting. "I can explain everything," he told them, trying to remain calm, remembering how easily their sibling rivalry often erupted into full-scale brawls. "There is so much you don't know about our family. Let's go inside, get Joe on the phone, and I'll tell you about it."

"Well, I don't know how this could be so danged important you had to wreck the place and get us altogether today," his older brother Jake complained. "Seems like you could have been a little more respectful."

"That's just about all the crap I'm taking from you two," Adam yelled. "What's up? I interrupt your naps or your golf games? Dammit, I've got the most important news you've ever heard, and you're acting as if it's too much trouble. Fine! I'm out of here."

"Oh. All right," Jake replied, anger still clouding his face. "I'm sorry. We'll listen, but this had better be good."

"It is. Now get your sorry asses inside, get Joe on the phone, and I'll tell you. If you can't tell from this bandage, I've got a concussion. Somebody shot at me and destroyed my car, and I'm more than a little pissed."

As soon as the brothers were in the kitchen, Ben poured each of them a glass of whiskey from a bottle he had brought in from his truck. After taking a drink, Adam told them of the great Roberts mystery, beginning with the fact they were the grandsons of notorious outlaws and how their grandfather came into possession of the land. He closed the historical portion of his presentation with the discovery of the journals and how their grandfather had blamed their grandmother for the murders.

Adam could tell from their expressions they thought he was a couple of beers short of a six-pack as he told them he had buried two skeletons he'd found under the lilacs out by the cottonwood tree. When he related how somebody had tried to destroy the bones by pulverizing them, shot at him, and burned down the cottonwood before hitting him over the head, they were openly skeptical. When Adam finished, the bottle was empty, Jake and Ben had a glassy-eyed stare, and he could hear Joe yelling for his wife to bring him a beer.

"Come on," Jake said, pushing himself away from the table. "I can accept we're related to rustlers, but murderers and skeletons? That's a little too much. And if grandma wrote journals, surely we would have read them by now.

"Why are you making all this up?"

"Well sport." Adam said. "I've got the journals stashed. You'll be able to see them tomorrow. But about the bodies, let's go upstairs, I bet we can find pieces of bone I missed when I cleaned up the mess. I was in too much of a hurry to have been real thorough."

"Aw shit," Ben swore thirty seconds after his brothers were in the room where Adam had laid the skeletons, holding up what could only have been a jawbone. "This is human, Jake. He's telling the truth. And look here's a finger bone, and this white dust. It's bone ain't it? Skeletons were under the rhubarb?"

"Boys," Adam announced while they were gawking at the bones in Ben's hands. "Now that we have the doubting Thomas shit out of the way, we have some issues to discuss, beginning with what we want to do about this, and who wants to keep it a secret."

Back in the kitchen, they finished Ben's whiskey and started working on the last of Adam's beer. The stress of family reunions, they joked, had always given them a predisposition to dipsomania. Learning their family's newly discovered history intensified the effect. Since Adam had called the meeting, he took the lead. "Joe, can you hear us? We're all back together."

"Yeah. I can hear you just fine. Jake, Ben? You guys find anything upstairs? Any evidence our brother hasn't gone completely nuts?"

"Uh. Yep. I wish we hadn't though," Ben cut in. "We found human bones and white, powdery dust all over. Just as Adam described. His story is real, and we've got a problem."

"Well, I don't know that we have a problem, Joe. This is Jake, if you can't recognize voices over the speaker. I don't see a problem. We just keep the story about the skeletons quiet and send Adam back to Boulder where he can blend in with the other spandex-wearing health-nuts. The rest of us can go back to our lives." Adam's brothers had always considered Boulder too trendy. His living there was a constant subject of great merriment.

"No. You're wrong, Jake," Adam said. "I thought the same thing at first. But I've been thinking it over. Let me tell you why I don't think we can cover it up - and it has nothing to do with a progressive lifestyle.

"We have a history as a family. My kids, your kids, our grandkids, they all deserve to know it. Good and bad happens in every family. What example does it set if we can't admit who we are? Also, as a historian, I know that Grandma's journals and the story of the Roberts are great discoveries. We can't let them go unstudied.

"I know this may be hard to explain, but let me try. I don't think our grandmother was the killer, even though she had to live the rest of her life with Grandpa thinking she was. I think that's why they assaulted me and burned the tree down. Somebody doesn't want me to discover who the real murderer was. We may have a chance to clear her name, and we should take it.

"Also, these kids, the murdered young people, they deserved more than this. They were living and breathing people with real hopes and fears. They deserve a chance to take their place in history."

"Yeah. Sure." Jake said, unleashing his cynicism. "And you know this how? Because of vandalism? I'll bet ghosts came and talked to you. You've probably been talking to the dead since you got here. When you see Grandpa, ask him exactly where he caught that thirteen-pound walleye. I been looking all over the lake and can't find it.

"No wonder they call where you live the Granola capital of Colorado. It's full of fruits and nuts, and you've adapted well. Let's just forget this and get back to our lives."

Joe, an engineer who the other brothers had teased about his dedication to empiricism, surprised them all with his reaction. "Jake, I hear you. I know what you're saying, but I agree with Adam. We can't let somebody run us off our own history. And what about Grandma? If she didn't do it, we need to prove it. We have a chance to clear her name and wherever she is, I think she'll know it."

"How will she? Don't tell me you believe this voodoo ghost crap too? What's the matter with you?" Jake stood up and pounded his fist on the table.

Joe's voice boomed over the speaker. "Enough Jake, enough. Now shut up. I'd like to read the journals. If they're everything Adam says, I think we should publish them. Look at it differently. This could be a wonderful opportunity. We'd be stupid to just walk away."

"Now just a cotton-picking minute," Jake pleaded. "Don't you guys care about Grandma and Grandpa, or Mom and Dad? Or me? I still have to live here. We are about to announce the biggest family secret in Nebraska. We literally have skeletons in our family closet. If Adam is wrong about the murderer, we could be giving our grandmother the reputation of murderess for eternity. No! Forget it. Nobody ever needs to know about any of this."

"Sorry, but I'm going to have to agree with Adam and Joe," Ben chimed in. "It's not right to leave this undone. I'm ready to take some time off and start. Jake, you're retired, you can help. How about you, Joe? Take a couple of days off and fly up. We'll pick you up in Denver or you can hop a small plane into Sidney. Let's figure this out."

"Good idea." Adam said, allowing anger to influence his tone. "I'm pissed off about everything that has happened since I've been here. I don't think you just let this violence happen without doing something about it.

"Consider another part of this, Jake. Remember when we got into a fight with our cousins in Sidney? Relatives we didn't know anything about then and still don't. You know it's all part of it. What happened here caused the split in our family. Don't you want to know what happened?"

"I sure as hell do," Joe yelled over the speakerphone.

"Jake, I'm going for it," Ben added. "All this secret mumbo jumbo is too much for me."

"I know when I'm outvoted, and you guys have never listened to what I've had to say. You just think I'm the older brother who stayed on the farm while you ran off to your fancy jobs somewhere else. Except for you, Ben, but you've been a loner since the war. So I'll go along. Let's find out what happened. On one condition! We won't release anything to the press, the police, or anybody else until we know the answers and all agree. Okay?"

They quickly made plans. Joe would fly into Sidney the next day and rent a car. Ben's wife was going to join him, and they would stay with Jake. Joe wanted to stay at the farm alone and see if he could detect any paranormal activity. He intended to bring a motion-operated video camera and a device that measured energy. If ghosts were there, he told the others, science would detect them. They closed by agreeing to meet for a barbecue at Jake's the following evening.

Finished with the first meeting of the remaining Roberts family, Adam drove back to Sidney in the old pickup after promising to rent a car and never drive the prized piece of junk again. The insurance adjuster had surveyed the damage to his car and said the company would pick up the cost of the rental car until he had a chance to buy another one. Adam didn't care what they did with the wreck sitting in the yard. They could leave it there as another monument to the Klan for all he cared.

Still exhausted after consuming too much alcohol, another ill-advised practice for head injury victims, Adam fell asleep as soon as he was in bed. He had just awakened and was dressing for dinner at ten o'clock when the phone rang. It was Cynthia; she was in the Ogallala hospital.

A car and a pickup, working in tandem, had forced her off the Interstate at the one place where the waters of the North Platte River bordered the highway. The pickup, tan with Sidney license plates, had slammed on its brakes in front of her, while the car passing her suddenly took a sharp right, almost running into her car. Instinctively, she had turned off the highway and into the river. Luckily, the Platte was wide and shallow, and her car came to rest sitting upright in three feet of water.

She was in the hospital for evaluation while her car was in a repair shop. Her son was on the way to pick her up. After she got back to Medicine Lodge, she would borrow her son's car and drive to Adam's motel the next morning.

Adam assumed her attackers were the people who'd been trying to frighten him away. They had been sending another message or else they had tried to kill her. Each time something happened these people intensified the violence. He and his brothers had to stop them. Someone was going to get hurt if they didn't.

CHAPTER SEVENTEEN

ADAM WALKED TO THE MOTEL'S RESTAURANT THE NEXT morning feeling better than he had since he'd found what remained of Jesus and Consuelo. His headache had faded to only a bad memory, and Cynthia had called. She was feeling great, not even stiff or bruised, and was going to leave for Medicine Lodge before nine o'clock.

She was safe, and even though he didn't know who had attacked her or him, at least he was no longer in this alone. He had something his grandfather didn't have when the Klan showed up to take Consuelo and Jesus. His family had joined the battle on his side, and this time the Roberts clan would stand together.

After eating, he walked to a bookstore and picked up a paperback novel featuring his favorite serial killer hunter. Adam didn't have anything to do until meeting his brothers that afternoon at Jake's house, and lying around sounded like a great plan. The rest of the morning he read, talked to Cynthia when she phoned, called his wife, and watched daytime television. For the first time since deciding to stay at his parent's old house and face his demons, he was a little bored.

About one o'clock in the afternoon, he picked up a rental Jeep Cherokee and drove to meet his brothers. Joe had arrived before noon, so he and Adam ate lunch at the Custom Harvester Lounge and Restaurant while they waited for Ben and Jake to finish playing golf. Adam remembered the cafe as the only place to eat in town. It was known as Fred's Watering Hole before the owner hired a cook and turned it into a restaurant.

It didn't matter what was going on, how serious anything was, or even where he was, you could always depend on Jake to play eighteen holes before getting down to work. The family joke for the last twenty years had been whether Jake could get St. Peter or the devil to wait until he putted-out on the eighteenth.

The brothers met on Jake's deck after the golfers returned. As part of a lost bet, Ben had to bring a case of Budweiser in long neck bottles. Just as in old times, they would settle the latest crisis over beer. As soon as they quieted down, Adam started the discussion.

"I'm glad you guys decided to help me with this. I'm tired of feeling like a target. I've told you everything that's happened to me. Now there's been something else. Cynthia Schmidt - maybe you guys remember her, she's about your age, Ben, her name was Larsen before she married Herb Schmidt - has been helping me. She's the director of the Medicine Lodge Museum and has a real interest in what I've found. Anyway, she was doing some research on the state computers in Lincoln for me yesterday. On the way home last night two cars forced her off the Interstate and into the North Platte down around Ogallala. She's okay, but she said it wasn't an accident. Somebody purposefully ran her off the road."

"I'm glad she's all right." Jake slammed his bottle down onto the table and jumped to his feet. "But I thought we were going to keep this in the family. Is she going to keep quiet? Who else knows?"

"I understand your feelings, Jake," Adam said, trying to adopt a conciliatory stance. "They're only natural. Only my wife and Cynthia know anything about this. Yes, Cynthia will keep it quiet, she's working with me. We can trust her, and her help has been invaluable. We're going to need her as we work through this."

"Of course, I remember her. Ran into her a couple of years back," Ben said, a huge smile lighting his face. "As I recall she's a fine looking woman. Didn't know you still had it in you. I bet she had to work real hard to get you straightened out."

"Oh! That was really funny. I don't even need to comment. Just trust me. She will keep this secret."

"And what else won't she tell?" Joe doubled over with laughter. "She won't tell her husband how many pills you had to take to get it up, is that it? I heard you even have to take Viagra to keep your left arm straight when you play golf. What'd she have to do, splint it up with Popsicle sticks?"

"No. She used toothpicks. She probably didn't have a big time," Ben added, breaking up Joe even more. Now even Jake was smiling and forgetting his anger.

The three of them smirked and carried on, finishing their first beer and telling more jokes before Adam could get them back onto their family history and whoever was trying to keep them from uncovering it. "Uncovering," Ben started laughing again. "We know what you've been uncovering."

Never mind that they were in a meeting about murders in the family, it was the first time they had all been together since their mother died. They turned the discussion into an adolescent game of finding hidden meanings and chugging beer until Jake threw his weight on the side of seriousness, telling Ben to shut up and Adam to get on with it.

"Here's what I figure," Adam said. "The first is that we need to can the word games. The second is that we need to decide about the release of our history. Who else are we going to have to talk to? Our families, especially our kids, deserve to be in on the decision. At least they need to know what's going on, but that's down the road a little.

"We need to find out who the killer was, and we have to find out who is trying to stop us. I believe the violence is escalating. The shot was a warning. Getting knocked out was painful, but they could have killed Cynthia last night. We're going to have to stop them before they kill somebody."

"I think you're right," Joe was taking notes again, determined to keep the brothers on task. "Tell us your theories about both. You've been working on this the longest. What do you think?"

"Aw, shit, Joe. He's going to tell us what the spooks told him," Jake said, glaring at his younger brothers. "Go ahead, Adam, but this time leave out the ghosts. Just tell us what you know."

Both Ben and Joe jumped up, as if Jake had accused them of preferring wine to beer. "No," they shouted simultaneously. "Tell us about the ghosts."

"I'll try to do both," Adam said. "Let's look at what we know about the murders. Our grandfather sent Grandma Sarah, our dad, Consuelo and Jesus down into the storm cellar while he waited in the front yard with rifles for the Ku Klux Klan to show up. We know from the journals the Klan got to the farm about the same time a big storm did; the cellar was dark and Jesus was afraid and wanted a light. The Klan was there to send Consuelo and Jesus back to California."

"Tell me about that," Jake interrupted. "I'm not a historian like you. I thought the K.K.K was against blacks in the South. Why were they in Nebraska after a couple of kids from California?"

"Good question, Jake. I guess I got ahead of myself. Most Americans don't know it, but the Klan was almost dead until the famous movie, *Birth of a Nation*, was adapted from the book, *The Clansman*, a historical romance featuring white-sheeted Klansmen protecting the virtues of southern womanhood during the reconstruction period.

"After seeing the movie, people flocked to join the secret organization. It reached its greatest membership during that time and was extremely popular in the Midwest. The Klan hanged, shot, and burned a black man in Omaha. The Invisible Empire - that's what they called themselves - elected the governor of Colorado in 1922, and the army even got into it with them during a dance in the Black Hills.

"The Klan was against just about everybody and everything that didn't trace its roots to Protestantism, America's earliest arrivals, puritanical morals, and temperance. They hated nonwhite Americans and anyone who worshipped in a Catholic Church or any other religion that wasn't protestant and Christian. They were equally against gambling, prostitution, bootlegging, stealing, graft, sex, adultery, and anything else stern-faced preachers didn't like.

"We know Consuelo and Jesus were Mexican-American and would have met the test of being nonwhite. I assume, even though I didn't find any crucifixes by their bodies, that they were Catholic. According to Grandmother Sarah, Jesus had a predilection for dressing in Consuelo's clothes. Grandma also wrote that our great-grandmother, Molly, called him a Mexican queer. Suppose for a minute he was a transvestite, and suppose his homosexuality became known. In that case, the two young Mexican-Americans popped to the top of any Klan member's charts.

"Hold it a minute." Joe was writing as quickly as he could. "I don't know about you guys. But I need a minute to consider all of this. You're saying the Klan was strong around here and hated these two kids. Do you think they meant to hurt them? Did you guys ever hear Grandma or Grandpa talk about this?"

"No. Our grandparents and even Dad, if he knew, kept this secret. But, Adam," Ben interjected. "I remember one time, years ago, when you were studying history, you asked Grandpa if he ever joined the Klan, didn't you? I think he said he went to a meeting because of the whiskey. Isn't that right?"

"Yeah. Grandma even wrote about his going and drinking with people opposed to booze. He thought it was a joke. But you're right, he did go."

"All right. So Nebraskans were in the Klan. They were after Mexicans and homosexuals, and they held this big deal at the house. But that doesn't prove anything," Jake charged. "You said our grandfather guarded the cellar door. Nobody else got in. He would have seen them, and Grandma was holding a big knife. It just seems to me that it could only have been her or our father, and he was only seven. You can't prove anything else."

"You're right." Adam smiled and nodded his head. "At this point, I can't prove anybody else did it. But look at a couple of other facts. One, there was another entrance. Behind the shelves in the basement there used to be a door into the cellar. Grandma described in her journals how Grandpa put it there for her to have an escape route if somebody invaded the house. It's cemented shut, Grandpa probably did it when he put down the steel and turned the cellar into a tomb, but it was an open door then.

"What if somebody else got into the house through the back door, went into the cellar through the basement, knocked Grandma and Dad out, and then killed Consuelo and Jesus? Remember, it would have been extremely dark. The killer probably carried the only light.

"Two," he continued, holding up his fingers to stress the point, "Consuelo and Jesus were afraid of George's brother, Autie. I got the impression from the journals that they feared bodily harm from him after Grandpa ran him off the place. What if Autie killed them? What would Grandma have done if he came in through the basement? I think she was fond of him as Grandpa's younger brother. She might have thought he was there to protect her, even though she knew he'd attended Klan meetings. And did I tell you? It was our grandfather's uncle that was most abusive of Consuelo and Jesus at the meetings. He was the spokesperson to get rid of them.

"Jake, I think those possibilities poke holes all through your argument that only our grandmother could have done it. I think they present enough reasonable doubt that you could get an acquittal in a modern trial. I can't say beyond a shadow of a doubt that she didn't do it. She might have. But somebody else could have also."

"What about the ghosts? Did Grandma really tell you something, or was Jake just mouthing off?" Joe asked?

"Well, uh. Jake guessed right. Not because he's intuitive or anything, but because he's a raging cynic. The other night at the farm, our grandmother came to me while I was asleep and said she didn't do it. Said she couldn't have."

"And you think that was real, tell them." Jake said, laughing uncontrollably. "I knew it. I just knew this was going to be another of your ghost stories."

"Boys," Adam told them after Jake finally quieted down, "I've seen ghosts since I was six or seven. I don't know if they are ghosts or figments of my imagination. I can't even tell you if I'm awake or dreaming when I see them. One of the reasons I came here was to find out which. But if you asked me right now and demanded I make a decision about them one way or the other, then Jake's right. Yep. I think there are ghosts. And I believe our grandmother Sarah told me she was innocent. I'm not asking you to believe me. So let's work through what else we know and leave my spooks alone."

"Jake, I've got to agree with Adam," Ben said, placing his hand on Adam's shoulder in a show of support. "You're talking plain old bullshit! I don't care whether you believe in ghosts or if Adam says they followed him to school, but he made damn good points about the possibility of somebody else doing the killing. You need to can your shit and listen. Go play golf if you can't get in the game."

"I agree. I flew all the way up here from Texas, and I'm not going to let your closed mind shut this down," Joe added, anger coloring his voice. "I don't think our grandmother was a killer, and I want to find out who was. Now, Adam, who do you think is behind the troubles you've had since you've been here?"

"That's the other piece of news we've got to discuss. Cynthia called me from Lincoln yesterday before she left. She found out our grandfather's younger brother, Autie, is still alive. He lives in a rest home in Okalahoma, but he's not there now. He checked out and has gone someplace else."

Jake stood slowly, as if he were listening to his over sixty-year-old bones creak with each motion, leaned against the railing of his deck, and looked out over the ridge of the north table silhouetted in the late afternoon sun. His demeanor had changed from that of a cynic to a man hurt by the secrets kept from him. "You mean to say we've got a great-uncle, over one hundred years old that knew this country when it was wild and untamed, a cowboy and kid outlaw, who is still alive? You honestly say that's true?"

"It's true, Jake," Adam said, placing his arm across his older brother's shoulders and walking with him back to his chair. "Brings it around full circle, doesn't it? Makes the past a part of us and our future."

Wiping away tears, his skin tanned and leathery from the Nebraska sun and wind, Jake looked like the brother Adam remembered as a star quarterback, goose hunter, and mentor. He spoke with more sensitivity than the others had ever heard from him before. "I always felt sorry, Adam," he whispered, "that I was never able to share your love of the history of this country. To me it was always farms, work, and home. A place to live, raise my kids, watch Nebraska football and all. It was just home.

"But now I feel so close to Mom and Dad and Grandma and Grandpa. I never told you guys how much I miss them, how I cried myself to sleep every night for a year after they were all gone. I felt as if something in me had died too. I put it off as being too emotional and tried to close up against it. There was so much I wanted to say to them, and so much I wanted them to say to me.

"I recognized awhile back that I didn't listen to them enough when we were kids, or even when you guys had gone away, and I was still here taking care of them. You with your big-shot lives and me here on the farm, taking care of Mom and Dad and driving the tractor.

"I don't know, call it wanting to know more about myself, my family, or even history. Probably I'm learning that's all history is, just something that gives us a sense of our identity and how we got to be. But I can't let this opportunity go. I have to meet Autie. Ask him about everything. Learn from him. About me. About us.

"Okay. I'm in," he continued. "But we're going to do this with some finesse. We just ain't declaring war. Let's go about it rationally, act as if we know what we're doing, and try to do this right. See if we can't bring our family back together."

The group hug - Ben, Joe, and Adam putting their arms around Jake's shoulder - was something none of them had ever experienced before. They were in it together, and each had a new sense of family, until Jake stiffened, shrugged off his brother's arms and announced, "Enough of this Boulder huggy-feely bullshit. No wonder we always kick your ass in football. Let's get to work."

"Adam, do you have any idea how old this guy, Autie, is anyway? Christ, he must be ancient," Joe asked as he started off for the bathroom.

"I think I remember reading in the journal he was ten when our great-grandfather was hanged in 1910. What? That would mean he was born in 1900, so I'd say he's about 105."

"We've got a relative who's more than one hundred years old that we've never heard of? You know, I've never thought this before, but I'm getting angry." Jake announced, his mind obviously still whirling with emotion. "We deserved to know our history, no matter how bad it was. How could they have kept this away from us?"

"I hear you," Ben said after thinking about it for a minute. "But I don't think Mom and Dad knew either. Grandpa could be a rough guy. Remember after the war, how Dad was working in California at a job he liked, but Grandpa told him he had to come out and take over the farm? Jake, you and Adam were alive then; I'll bet you probably even remember the move. I'll bet if Dad asked why, Grandpa told him it was none of his business. The way Grandpa was then, Dad wouldn't have thought anything about it."

"Be that as it may, and I may need another beer." Reaching over and grabbing each brother a fresh bottle, Joe brought up a point that had been bothering Adam. "My first thought is that Autie is the one behind what's been going on, but he's way too old to go around drinking beer, shooting out windows, setting trees on fire, and hitting Adam over the head. He can't be doing this alone."

"That's another reason I'm angry and thinking about this whole other side of our family," Jake announced. "Adam, we never did know why our so-called cousins attacked us almost fifty years ago. Suppose it wasn't because of anything we'd done, and it wasn't a school rivalry as we thought. Do you imagine it could have been because they were raised to hate us? The other side of our family kept the hatred alive? My guess is that Autie is in Sidney and our own cousins, people with the same last name, are behind this."

Emptying his most recently opened beer, Joe studied his notes a moment before speaking. "Well! Let me see now. Here's where I am and what I think we need to do. Jake, I expect you're right. The bone-crushers and tree-burners are these guys from Sidney you call our cousins, I'd never even heard of them before tonight, and they're helping Autie. We're going to have to find out what kind of people they are, where they live, and if Autie's with them. What about this tan pickup? We'd be a lot closer to the truth if we knew one of them had a truck such as that.

"I'll tell you what. Since I work with computers and the net all the time, I'll go on-line with Jake's machine and find out all the information there is about those two. Jake, surely you know somebody who knows them. This whole state isn't that big, they still call it a small town with long streets. Talk to somebody who can tell you about them. Find out if anyone's seen an old man hanging around them.

"Adam, you get your new girlfriend working on Autie. Have her call back to the land of the Okies and find out where he went and what he's like. Ben, why don't you get a Sidney phone book, I'm sure Jake has one, and see if there are any Roberts listed in Sidney. If there are, get the address and drive up there to see where they live. See if you can find a tan pickup or an old guy sitting out in the shade remembering when he was a famous outlaw.

"That ought to about do it. How about we meet for dinner tomorrow night at Adam's motel and put all this info together?"

"Sounds like a great plan." Relieved that somebody else was making plans and taking the lead, Adam had only one statement left to make. "But she's not my girlfriend. I'll get reservations to eat about seven."

———

Adam barely beat the woman he'd protested wasn't his girlfriend back to his motel room. She looked beautiful as she walked into the room, and he knew once again he had no ability to tell her to go away. Her kiss was as soft as newly fallen snow; he didn't want it to stop, or ever to let go of her. When she pulled away, he saw laughter in her eyes.

"What's so funny," he asked, thinking it must be his swift arousal.

"I know something you don't," she giggled as if she were thirteen and keeping a secret from her best friend.

"Well, what is it?" He asked, leading her over to the bed.

"Just that your great-uncle Autie is not only alive, he's right here in Sidney. He's not more than a mile away from where we are. How do you like that?"

"I don't like it nearly as much as I do holding you." Pulling her down onto the bed beside him, Adam traced the outline of her face with his fingers. "Besides, we figured that out. I bet Brother Ben is sitting outside the house where he is at right now. He's also looking around for a tan pickup."

"How did you know? Who's he staying with? When I called the rest home they wouldn't tell me. In fact they said they couldn't tell me anything, but I got it out of them by saying I wanted to tape-record him for the museum."

Adam had to fill her in on the rest of his family. "We've got two cousins living here in town. They have the same last name and everything. They're the great-grandsons of our great-grandfather's brother. He was Autie's uncle who showed up at the ranch with Molly and helped her keep the family tradition of rustling alive. They lived in Medicine Lodge when we were little, but they went to high school here. You ever hear of them?"

"Well, yes! I've heard of the Roberts here in town, but I didn't know they're related to you. Your family was always so well respected. Everything I've ever heard about them is just the opposite. They've been in jail, and they're always drunk. People around here are afraid of them. I'm sorry, but they known as bad people."

"Yeah. We figured that out already. My brothers and I are going to get together here tomorrow night for dinner. Want to join us and meet them? By the way, they call you my new girlfriend anyway. I protested and acted insulted, but I don't think they believed me."

"I would love to meet them, and I don't care what they call you or me. It's none of their business, although they do sound like they know you awfully well or else they're a bunch of gossipy old women."

Adam murmured, "They don't know me at all," as he gently rolled her onto her back.

Her response was warm, endearing, and enthusiastic.

CHAPTER EIGHTEEN

"BYE, TIGER," CYNTHIA PURRED AS SHE WAS LEAVING. Adam was still in bed, trying to go back to sleep. "You be sure to take your vitamins or whatever it is you guys take at times such as this. I'll be back tonight to make sure you're still up for this little affair."

It was funny, but he didn't feel too old anymore. Adam was thoroughly enjoying himself and was no longer merely the recipient of her affection. He returned it just as strongly. He guessed it was his one last hurrah. He hadn't gone looking for it, and didn't consider himself a dirty old man, but he never looked most gift horses in the mouth either.

Adam didn't know what else to do during the day. Cynthia had already told him everything he needed to find out as his part of the investigation. He decided to call Joe and ask him how his first night alone in the old house had been.

His youngest brother was affable, but barely awake. "Oh, Adam. Good morning. How are you? What's up? Did your girl leave early? Not enough power in the old blue pill to get you a morner?"

"Very funny, Joe. Actually I was calling to see how your night went. Mine was just fine, thank you. Did anything happen? Your fancy machines detect any movement or energy? Grandma or Consuelo come to see you? Oh, that's right. No women ever do look you up at night, do they?"

"Now don't be nasty, big brother," Joe retorted. "I'm just teasing you a little. You can take it. But to answer your first question, no. No energy. No movement and no sightings, but you said your first night was the same. And as for your second question, a gentleman never tells.

"But I do have to tell you. I don't know if it's because the place has been empty, because you put skeletons upstairs, or because I'm hypersensitive, but something is different here than it used to be. The house is too quiet. Not like its deserted, more like it's dead. The stairs don't creak. I don't hear the wind or anything. I don't remember it ever being this quiet. I've got to tell you it's spooky. I'm freaked."

Adam told him his experiences had been the same. First he had felt the quiet and then the ghosts, or dreams, came. When he asked if he should drive out and stay with him, Joe responded that it was something he had to do alone.

After wandering down to the café for coffee, Adam went back to his room. Since there were no sights he wanted to see, nothing sounded better than reading a good book. He'd just fluffed up the pillow and settled in with the murder mystery when the phone rang. Ben spoke in hushed tones as conspirators do in bad movies.

"Adam," he whispered. "You've got to come down to Medicine Lodge right away. Cynthia may be in trouble. I need help."

"Okay. Okay. Tell me where to find you and what the deal is. Wait. Give me your cell phone number. I'll call you as soon as I'm on the road."

Five minutes later, he was out of town on the Interstate and dialed Ben's number.

"Hello, Adam? I'm glad you called. Where are you?"

"Heading your way at over one hundred. I'll be there in ten minutes. Where are you and what's going on?"

"I'm parked behind the old airplane hanger. He can't see me."

"Ben, for God's sake. If he can't see you he certainly can't hear you. Don't whisper. Just tell me who he is and what's going on."

Ben's voice grew a little louder, as if a secret agent were no longer standing beside him. "I drove to Sidney early this morning to start watching our cousins. According to the phone book there are two of them, Earl and Wilbur. Earl lives with their mother and everything was quiet around their house. I got to Wilbur's trailer court just in time to see him drive away in a tan pickup . . ."

"Tan pickup," Adam interrupted. "That about proves it. That's the guy who ran Cynthia off the road. It's probably the same truck that left tracks in our trees when he shot at me. Way to go, my man."

"No wait, that's not all. I followed him out to the farm. He drove up and down the road a couple of times just looking the place over. Then I followed him down here, in town. He's parked on a side street where he can see the museum. He's sitting in his car smoking. I've got the binoculars on him. Wait! Now he's pulled out a phone, he's dialing and calling somebody. Something's going on. You've got to get here right away."

Adam was within five miles of town and hadn't passed a car yet. "I'll be there in a couple of minutes. I'm going to hang up and drive faster. He won't recognize the Jeep I'm driving, I hope. I'll meet you in back of the hanger."

"Take it easy," Adam said when he jumped into Ben's car. "He's not going to do anything in daylight. And if he does, that's why I've been carrying this old 20-gauge around with me. We'll sit here and watch him."

"Come on, Adam," Ben replied, shaking with silent laughter. "After the jungles, this doesn't scare me. I only thought you should have the honor of saving your girlfriend. After all, you're the one who's going to get the reward. Besides, if she saw me, it would be all over for you."

"Very funny! I'm glad that having the crap scared out of you hasn't interfered with your warped sense of humor," Adam retorted, probably because he was the one worrying.

They sat in Ben's car for another thirty minutes watching their cousin watch the museum. Suddenly, their relative started the pickup and drove away as cautiously as any other farmer would in a small town. Ben said he would follow him and told Adam he'd better go see how his latest conquest was doing. Adam made an obscene gesture and hurried to the museum. Cynthia's peals of laughter met him at the door.

"Oh! You should've heard this. I thought I'd die laughing. When I answered the guy back saying, 'Frankly my dear, I don't give a damn,' I thought he was going to have apoplexy. I should have been an actress. I'm so good. At the least, a stand-up comedian." Cynthia wiped away tears of mirth while Adam stood there dumbfounded. "I know you don't know what I'm talking about. I'll tell you, and then tell me why you're here. Couldn't stay away, huh?"

He grabbed her by her shoulders, shaking them to gain her attention. "I'm here because you were in trouble. You don't know it, but a guy in a tan truck, I'm sure the one that ran you off the road, was outside. Ben and I thought he was going to hurt you. He just now drove away. Ben followed him."

"Aren't you the sweetest thing," she whispered, covering her mouth with her hands to still her laughter. "I knew he was out there. I watched him through the window as he watched me. He even called me up! He called me up and threatened me."

"Threatened you? What did he say? We'd better call the police." Adam couldn't take anymore threats. One of these days they would carry through with one and hurt or kill somebody. He didn't want it to be her.

"Call the police? Oh no, you big dummy. It wasn't that kind of a threat. He wasn't going to beat me up or kill me or anything. He said he was going to call my husband and tell him I spent the night with you in your motel. He must have been watching you and saw me. Isn't that a riot?"

"Yeah. That's about as funny as a heart attack. This guy is threatening to tell your husband you've been cheating on him, and you think it's funny? Damn Cynthia, but I can just imagine your husband calling my wife. I hoped this was our little secret."

"That's what's so funny, you dope," Cynthia was still laughing. "First of all, my husband wouldn't believe it. He's too macho to think I could possible want anybody else after him. I know him too well! He'd think that somebody was laughing at him. He'd get mad and go after the guy playing a joke on him."

"Sure. I imagine most women in your position want to believe that. But it seems like a mighty shaky thought to put much stock in. It wouldn't surprise me if your husband comes gunning for both of us."

Her laughter still didn't quit. "I suppose you could be right, though I don't think you are. You know why I recommended that motel, why I made sure you stayed there? Because my best friend owns it. She knows all about you and our little rendezvous, and she thinks it's great. I stay with her all the time, sometimes every night while the great white hunter is out with his buddies chasing poor, defenseless animals. My being there is about as ominous as my working late hours here, which I always do. Relax. I'm not just some little airhead.

"And while I don't mean to frighten you. You have nothing to do with this, other than you have shown me there is a chance for happiness. I'm leaving him. I've already got a unit at the motel, one that's equipped as an apartment. I've been thinking about it for months. It's time to enjoy my freedom and meet the man of my dreams."

She had obviously noted the stricken look on his face, the look that said she couldn't be serious, and that he didn't need a lonely divorcee hounding him in the future. "Will you get over yourself," she said while staring into his eyes. "You are my one Great Affair while I'm married, but you aren't the man of my dreams. The man of my dreams doesn't have a wife waiting for him.

"Maybe if you drive down from Colorado another time, sometime in the future when all this business is over, when you come to see the displays and Sarah's journals, maybe you'll still have privileges, but I'm not sure. I do know that as soon as you're gone, you are only going to be an old friend fondly remembered.

"But, I would like to enjoy my Great Affair a little longer. Now get out of here and let me work. Get plenty of rest. I plan to entertain you in my new apartment after we talk to your family tonight. That way they won't be able to accuse you of entertaining me in your room."

CHAPTER NINETEEN

ADAM DIDN'T SPEND THE AFTERNOON RESTING OR WORRYING about how many pills he needed to hold up his end of the affair. He wanted to understand the past, and that meant following the trails his grandparents had walked when they first showed up in western Nebraska. He was going to find the remains of the Medicine Lodge Cattle Company, which he'd never heard of before. Then he would pay a visit to one of his favorite hunting areas when he was in high school, the Bull Horn Creek Cattle Company.

The house and barns of the ranch where his grandmother had worked were gone, as was all local memory of what had been a large enterprise. On the lonely banks of Medicine Lodge Creek, he found two stone chimneys. One had been on each end of the big house, standing as a plains Stonehenge, monuments to a time gone by. The cookhouse, separated from the foundation of the big house by less than ten feet, was full of junk. The ovens Sarah and the children had used to help cook Christmas dinner were gone, probably now displayed as accent pieces in multimillion dollar homes.

However, it didn't look as if very much had changed on the Bull Horn Creek Cattle Company. The ranch foreman and his family lived in the rock and log house where Gurley had died in his mother's arms. Under a huge tree at the base of a high sandstone cliff, looking out over a lush pasture full of Black Angus cattle and a myriad of ponds covered with ducks and geese, he found Gurley's grave. An elaborate tombstone he had never noticed before marked the young man's well-tended, final resting place.

Adam could see why his grandfather thought this was the most beautiful place he'd ever seen. It had a different beauty than the Rockies, but it was just as striking. As a boy, Adam had hunted Bull Horn's ducks, geese, and deer every chance he had, but he had never really seen it before. He must have traipsed through the gully where Cowboy George rescued Gurley from the longhorn. He wished he had known then. He wished his grandfather had told him his Old West adventure stories.

Gazing over unchanged vistas, seeing it as it had been when it was wild country, an overwhelming sense of history struck Adam. He'd always tried to give his students and his children a sense of history - a sense of the familiarity each should have with their past.

He had always told his students that the beauty, the majesty, and the sweep of human experience made up the stuff of history. Sure, they learned dates, battles, concepts, politics, and important events - most of the facts taught and tested in traditional courses. But what he wanted them to know, the singular most important point to learn, was that people of the past were no different than those of the present.

Hopes, dreams, fears, wishes, hormones, urges, and needs had remained the same through the generations. He told his classes that premarital sex had always been a reality. In the past, except for possibly some stilted Victorians and the Puritans, it was more normal than not. Extramarital sex? Of course their ancestors participated.

Why else had prostitution been legal and profitable for so much of human history?

People had always wanted more for their children than they had, and they had always wanted others to like, respect, and admire them. No one in history had ever wanted to live in shame or to have people point them out in public. People of today are as people have always been.

And then he knew. He was willing to bet anything there was an attraction between Jesus and Autie. Perhaps they had even acted on their impulses. That or something similar had happened between the young cowhand and the gentle boy that brought the cowboy's macho gunfighter mentality into question. Perhaps he had found Jesus dressed as Consuelo, thought it was the woman he loved, and exposed his love, and himself, to a man.

Autie's hatred, undiminished after more than eighty years, was that of a tormented soul, a man who had never been able to accept himself. Adam would bet Autie had never married and his life had been one of guilt, anxiety, and pain. He had killed Jesus and Consuelo to ensure their silence and to try to find some peace.

Worried that discovery of the bodies would implicate him, Autie must have had someone watching the farm secretly for years. He found out Adam had discovered the tomb and figured the search would lead back to him. He couldn't let that happen.

Adam drove back to his motel, reflecting on his theory, convinced he was correct. No other explanation would account for keeping the fires of hate ablaze for so long. Now was the time for his family to help their great-uncle let it go. There had been enough punishment; eighty years of fear and self-loathing had been a harsh sentence. Sending a 105-year-old man to jail for a crime he committed in another lifetime would not serve justice. It was a time for healing, not incrimination.

The brothers met in the restaurant of Adam's motel, but again he was the last to arrive. He had been on the phone with his wife in Boulder. Her project was proceeding well; they were adapting chemicals in an existing formula she was sure the City Council would approve. He told her not to count on it. Any governmental agency that passed statutes against moving plague-carrying prairie dogs and had abolished human ownership over animals, making people their guardians, would be a tough sell for anything that killed a living creature - even mosquitoes.

As he walked to the table, Cynthia was charming his siblings. "Well, I see you've all met," he said. "I'm sure you told her all your little jokes. The only good to come out of this is that she is now able to see which one of us is really the nicest, smartest, and handsomest."

"How true," Ben said, a beer in one hand, massaging the back of Cynthia's neck with the other. "She's already asked why she couldn't work with me instead of you."

"Yeah. Well, working with her would interfere with my golf game, so I told her to stick with you," Jake said around a mouthful of chips and salsa.

Only Joe was quiet. He had three empty beer bottles in front of him and the fourth held less than a swallow. "What's with you," Adam asked. "Won't the other little boys let you join in their games?"

"I thought I'd wait until everybody was here before I said anything. I don't know what it is, but I went out to the farmhouse to change my clothes and clean up before I came here. I can't describe it, but I'm almost afraid to go back. I know it sounds weird, but it's spooky out there.

"The house is too quiet. When I'm inside I can't hear anything, not even the wind. I'm telling you it's unnatural. I'm going back, but I'm scared to death."

Jake exploded when he found he had another brother with sensitivity to the supernatural. "Oh Hell!" he thundered. "Now I suppose Grandma is going to come and see you tonight. You're as bad as Adam. I lived there for twenty years after you guys were gone. I never felt or saw anything out of the ordinary."

"I think it's because they know." Adam had been thinking about the manifestations, and it was the only explanation that made sense. "The spirits in the house know Autie is back, that we are looking into their deaths, and that something is going to happen. If they reveal themselves to Joe at anytime Jake, you're going to have to start considering they're real."

"Well, I only know that I'm not staying out there," Ben said. "I have no wish to see old women with knives. Thank you very much. I'm staying with Jake. I don't need any this. I've got a load of ghosts of my own, all from Southeast Asia."

"See what it's like to be in this family, Cynthia," Adam tried to make everyone comfortable. "We fight and argue, but we work well together. Jake's the most skeptical. Joe is an analytical engineer, it's surprising he notices the supernatural and Ben, well, Ben . . ."

"I can talk for myself. I want to get this over with and get my fishing pole back in my hands. I've had my fill of fighting bad guys and battling strange beings from the beyond. Cynthia, I'm the nicest one. You'll find me the most agreeable."

"Oh, I think you're all just fine. I'm glad I got to see all of you again. I think I've talked to each of you at one time or another. I just wanted to say that everybody remembers your mom and dad as the nicest people in the world. We were all so proud of them when they were the elected royalty at Old Settlers. Everyone felt bad when they passed so suddenly. You must be very proud of them."

"We are, thanks," Adam said, taking over again. "Why don't we order, and then we can start talking about what we've discovered. I think I've figured out what's going on. It's just a theory, but it fits. . . ."

"Before you start into some long-winded tirade or something," Jake interrupted. "You should know we already ordered, and for you also. It was Cynthia's idea. She's a good friend of the owner. They're going to serve us fried chicken, mashed potatoes and gravy, corn on the cob, and ice-cream sundaes family style. So let's get down to it. I've got a tournament that starts early in the morning."

"Sounds good," Adam said, "I'll hold onto my theory until the end of the meeting. Why don't you start Jake? Did you talk to anybody who knows our relatives?"

"I talked to a couple of guys. Funny deal is, nobody thinks we're related to them even though we have the same last name. I can't find anybody who knows them very well. It seems they're more known by reputation than anything. We've got two second cousins living here. One has a house on the west end along the creek, that's Earl. The house was their parents. Their father has been dead for forty years. I guess he was a real boozer. Their mother, Amanda, is still alive and lives with Earl. The other is Wilbur. He stays in a trailer out in the Buffalo Trailer Court on the south side.

"According to the folks I spoke with, neither of them graduated from high school. Earl spent time in the pen, most of it for robbery and breaking into houses. He's pretty shiftless. It's a good thing his mom paid-off their house years ago. Earl spends most of his time watching television. He works part-time as a hired man for an old farmer west of town. I don't know anything about Amanda, she's more or less a shut-in.

"Wilbur, on the other hand, hasn't been out of the Wyoming pen very long. He did twenty years in Rawlins for rape. Beat a young woman up pretty bad. Kept her as his punching bag and sex slave in a trailer for over a week until she managed to escape. People around there remember it as atrocious. He's vicious and mean. I think Earl follows him around.

"We need to be careful dealing with these two guys. They're a couple of powder kegs waiting to blow."

"What about Autie? Any evidence he's in town?" Joe asked right before he ordered another beer. If he didn't slow down with the alcohol, Adam was afraid his youngest brother would never make it back to the farmhouse to watch for ghosts.

"Nobody I talked to knows. That's what I mean about them. They aren't neighborly. The good people of Sidney go out of their way to avoid them. I doubt if anybody in town knows if he's here."

"He is." Ben broke in. "I've told you guys, and I assume Adam told Cynthia, about following Wilbur out to the farm and down to the museum today. When he left, I followed him back to Sidney. He stopped at Earl's and went into the backyard. I snuck down the alley and looked between the slats in the wood fence. Sitting in the back under a tree, smoking a hand-rolled cigarette, was the oldest person I've ever seen. Had a cane beside him, but he got up without using it to greet Wilbur. He looks old, but he's spry.

"You know, this is terrible to say about our relatives, but neither Wilbur nor Earl looked right. I don't know how to say it, but they looked wrong. Like they, uh. I don't know. I guess they just look mean and angry. Almost as if you watched them long enough, you'd see insanity."

"All right. Now we're cooking." Adam said. "We know about Earl and Wilbur and that Autie is in town. Joe, were you able to find anything else out about them on the net?"

"Nothing different. But I can embellish a little. I found newspaper articles and court reports on Lexis about the rape in Wyoming. Seems our cousin held the state reputation for meanness until those two guys killed that gay kid in Laramie. Wilbur horribly disfigured the woman he kept prisoner. She hasn't been mentally right since it happened. People were upset when they paroled him. I think they'd be happy to take him back and throw the switch.

"Earl seems to be real slow. He's never held a full-time job, and the army rejected him in the early seventies, if you can believe that. As far as I can tell, he hasn't had a driver's license for ten years. I don't know how he gets away with it since he must drive, but he doesn't care about much. He lives off the pension his mother gets for working so many years at the Sioux Army Depot.

"Their father, Vern, was the son of Roy and Rosie Roberts. Roy was our grandfather's uncle and that makes Vern grandpa's cousin, except he was much closer to Dad's age. Roy and Rosie had a farm along the creek south of Medicine Lodge where Vern and his brother, Will, he's dead now too, lived when they were boys."

"Want to hear about Autie now?" Cynthia asked, "I think it ties right in with the rest of this."

Their food arrived just as she started to speak. "Let's pass this around. As soon as everybody gets some, Cynthia will tell us about Autie. Is that all right with you guys?" Adam was already piling food on his plate as he spoke.

Within three minutes of filling their plates, the Roberts brothers were chowing down while Cynthia told them what she knew about Autie. "Through records, the Internet, calling colleagues who looked in old newspapers, and talking to an administrator at the rest home, I managed to piece together a lot of information.

"Your uncle's namesake was General Custer, Autie was his nickname. Autie Roberts is proud of that and tells everybody. His mother, Molly, this is what he told the people in the rest home, was the daughter of an Indian trader in Montana. She was about seven years old at the time of the Little Big Horn and was a great admirer of the general.

"By the way, I checked with the *Cody Enterprise*, the newspaper in a town near Meeteetse, Wyoming, and there is a record of a barn burning down that killed ten prize bulls and a couple of cowboys in 1910. According to the report, they were looking for some kid who'd had been with an outlaw the cowboys had hanged.

"Autie spent most of his life cowboying and drinking. He was never in serious trouble with the law, but he does have several arrests for fighting and public intoxication on his record. From when he was about thirty until he retired, he worked on one of the world's largest cattle ranches in Texas. I guess the ranch owners loved him. They still take care of him. One article described him as a real loner who stayed out in a line shack most of the time by himself. He only went to town to drink, and then he'd always get in a fight.

"He had a woman friend in town. She was Mexican. Never did become a citizen. People always assumed they would marry eventually, but they never did. She died right before he retired, but they had been together for almost forty years.

"According to the rest home administrator, the ranch paid his bills. He never has any visitors, except for Wilbur and Earl or their mother, Amanda. One of them goes to see him once a year. Usually it's just Amanda, I suppose that's because both Earl and Wilbur are usually in jail. He's never been any trouble at the rest home and always stays by himself, except one time he became so violent they had to sedate him."

Cynthia paused to take a drink, but Jake was so taken by it all that he urged her to keep going.

"Okay. Here it is," she continued. "He was watching television, something he almost never does. He calls it the devil's box. A program came on about transvestites fooling straight men into thinking they're women. The transvestites went on the program to confess to their lovers or something. Anyway, Autie went bananas. He threw his cane through the television set, started screaming at everyone in the place, and even attacked one of the nurses when the guy tried to restrain him. Except for the occasional rodeo on ESPN, he's never watched television since, and they haven't had any more trouble."

Now it was Adam's turn, and his theory about Autie and why he'd murdered Consuelo and Jesus meshed with Cynthia's discoveries. "I spent the afternoon at the former location of the Medicine Lodge Cattle Company where our grandmother worked before she married Grandpa. Almost everything is gone. I found a couple of rock chimneys, the cookhouse is still there, and you can see the outlines of a foundation but that's about it. No memories, nothing to suggest we have any connection there."

"Oh come on. What are you doing, searching new places for ghosts? At least you're consistent."

"Stay with me, Jake, I'll get there. I wasn't looking for ghosts. I was trying to find reasons for what happened. All I'm saying is that there's nothing along the Medicine Lodge Creek to help.

"Bull Horn Creek is different. When you read Sarah's journals about Grandpa and how much he loved the area - you have to drive out to Bull Horn. Block out the modern tractors, cars, and other signs of technology, and you're back in the west of Cowboy George's day. Cattle and horses as far as the eye can see. Ponds covered with mallards and Canadians, deer roaming the canyons. I had forgotten how beautiful it is. I never noticed it before, and I'll bet you guys didn't either because we weren't looking, but the boy's grave stands at the foot of a bluff where his parents buried him after Grandpa brought him home to die.

"I've always taught that to understand history, you must experience it where it happened. To understand the Holocaust you have to smell the shoes in the museum, touch the battered suitcases the victims packed their meager belongings in on their fateful trip to the chambers, and you need to walk through the camps. That's what I did with our grandfather's and his younger brother's lives. I went to a place they both lived and, I think, loved.

"Looking across those canyons and meadows, wondering exactly where young Cowboy George became a hero, I believe I figured out why Consuelo and Jesus were so afraid of Autie and why he killed them. All the clues are in Sarah's journals. I don't think she ever figured it out, at least not while she was writing. Remember she was a daughter of the Victorians, and Jerry Springer and MTV weren't around to remind of her of the human capacity for veniality.

"Consuelo Vargas was a beautiful young woman. Now use your imagination here. I don't know if it was lust or love, but let's consider the times and the heart of a young cowpoke and say Autie had fallen for her. He was only about seventeen. Even you old farts can remember what that was like. He probably thought about her all the time. The way she looked, walked, spoke, danced - everything she did went directly to his heart.

"And then let's imagine he had an assignation with her, that's a meeting or rendezvous for our culturally deprived siblings, and he went to it with love in his heart.

"Now let's imagine he discovers, maybe even after more such meetings . . ."

Gasping, Cynthia had figured it out. "Adam! It wasn't Consuelo was it? It was Jesus! Sarah wrote that he loved dressing in his sister's clothes and looked just like her when he did. Molly even called him a Mexican queer. Autie found out Jesus was taking his sister's place!

"Did Sarah know?"

"Interesting question," he said, and one he hadn't considered. "I don't know if she did at the time, but she must have later. Remember how Sarah described Jesus and Consuelo holing up in their room for several days. She heard crying. When she asked, Consuelo said everything was fine and to leave them alone.

"I'll bet it wasn't Consuelo crying. It was Jesus. He had fallen in love with Autie who rejected him, maybe even violently pushed him away. He was heartbroken. Not only that, it was about the same time Grandpa ran Autie, his mother, and his aunt and uncle off the ranch. Jesus would never see Autie again. He would never be able to reconcile with his love, a lover who butchered him and his sister a couple of years later."

Joe, busy taking notes as usual, was so far into the discussion he even raised his hand to speak. "I understand what you're saying, Adam. But Autie and the rest left the ranch in 1917." He paused while he checked the dates.

"The murders happened in 1920, three years later. That's a long time to carry so much anger. Wouldn't he have killed them a lot sooner? I mean, wouldn't time heal the wounds a little?"

"If hatred and anger were the only reasons, but they weren't." Ben interjected. "He was afraid someone would find out he'd had a homosexual relationship. Even if he innocently had thought it was Consuelo, people wouldn't believe his explanation. He killed them to shut them up. Didn't he?"

"That's how I figure it. Sadly, it's understandable. Remember, Autie lived during rough-and-tumble times when men were men and women stayed in the house and had babies. The fear of discovery must have slowly driven him crazy."

"You know," Jake said, almost in a whisper. "We've got a couple of jobs ahead of us, not the least of which is to get through to Autie and convince him no one will ever know, that we won't let anything soil his reputation. Do you realize that after eighty-years he still has an obsessive fear of discovery? His life must have been terrible. So afraid, and I bet feeling so guilty. Not to mention losing Consuelo, his first and, seemingly, unrequited love. It's not hard to understand his attraction to the Hispanic woman in Texas."

His brothers agreed. Joe told them he recorded it in his notes as their number one task. If they could make Autie rest easier, they had to try. "That's settled, Jake. What else do you think we need to do?" Ben asked, while trying to get an overloaded spoon of chocolate sauce dripping ice cream to his mouth.

"Well, obviously we need to decide what to do about Earl and Wilbur," Jake said, reaching over to help Ben wipe up spilled chocolate. "They don't sound like the kind we'll ever have reunions with, and I don't care about them. But how can we ignore them after all they've done? We need to get them off our backs. You want to turn them over to the law or take care of them ourselves?"

Adam had been the primary victim, and they looked to him for direction. "No law. As far as the insurance company knows unknown vandals wrecked my car. I don't have to help the police do their job.

"I want them to get the message this is over. I don't want any more violence. I don't need retribution. It's just over. They can go back to jail for all I care. I want them to leave Cynthia and us alone, and I think I know how to get it done."

Adam had worked his plan out when he had been alone in his room. It was another reason he had been late to the meeting. He'd even made notes so he wouldn't forget anything. "Let's use the knowledge we have to trap them. We should be able to lure Autie, Earl, and Wilbur into an isolated place where we can get the drop on them. Because of their proclivity towards violence, we'll need weapons. Here's what we do.

"Cynthia, you call Autie, and tell him you've been using me. He'll take the call. He has to be a bright old guy to control this. Tell him you have the journals and know what happened. Of course, you have to play the part of a conniving gold digger. Tell him you'll meet him someplace safe and give the journals to him. In return, you want full rights to publish an edited version along with his personal story.

"Make it seem like you see this as your ticket to a higher paying job with a major museum. You want out of Medicine Lodge, and he's going to help you.

"What do you guys think?" Adam was so sure his plan was perfect nobody would find any fault. But Ben surprised him.

"It's thin!" he announced, upending his beer and licking foam off his lips before continuing. "The payoff's not big enough. She needs to get more out of this. I don't think publishing and going to a bigger museum is enough of an enticement for double-dealing."

"Then you don't understand my business," Cynthia assured him. "I know people who would kill for this chance. This is a ticket to the History Channel for heaven's sake. I don't know if your cousins are smart enough to know that, but I'll bet Autie is. The people at the rest home told me television stations and historians are always trying to get an interview with him, but he'll never see them. Now we know why. Yes, Adam. This will work."

"I don't like it at all, but I'll bet I'm outvoted. You can be damn sure I'm bringing my rifle," Jake grumbled. "Where and when?"

Adam also had this figured out. "The most deserted place I can think of, and one that should appeal to Autie, is at the base of the butte where your first drive onto Bull Horn Creek Land and Cattle Company property. You know, where the creek bends around the butte, where we were always able to jump ducks.

"If they would agree to meet her there, one of us could be on the bluff, a couple in the trees by the creek, and one hiding in the willows around the pond. What do you think?"

Putting his pen down and stretching cramped muscles in his writing hand, Joe was the first to see a problem. "It's too damn far and too deserted. You're going to ask a really old guy to ride nearly forty miles in a car, twenty of them over bad roads, and go to a place Cynthia has no business knowing about anyway. I wouldn't believe her if she asked me to meet her there for a date."

Cynthia was quick to agree. "Adam, he's right. I would never ask someone to meet me in a place like that."

"Well then, Cynthia, where would you set up such a meeting?" Ben asked. "It needs to be in a place where we can overpower them without a fight. Where do you suggest?

Jake suddenly jumped up and started shouting. "I know. I know. I know the perfect place." And then he sat down smiling, as if he were waiting for his brothers to beg him to share his wisdom.

"Well, are you going to tell us?" Cynthia asked. "Or do you want us to guess?"

"Sure," Adam said. "Tell us, Most Wise One. Where is the Perfect Place?"

"Don't you see? Where it all happened. The farm. Meet them at the farm tomorrow night. All Cynthia needs to do is call them in the morning from the museum; it's not far from where she works and makes the most sense."

"No it doesn't," Joe announced. "I hate to interrupt your perfect moment of wisdom, Exalted One, but I'm staying out there, and they know it. Ben followed Wilbur there one day."

"Shit," Jake muttered.

"I was going to suggest the Museum," Cynthia said. "They know it's where I would be. It will be after hours, and it's right on the highway. Autie doesn't have to make a long drive on rough roads, and it will be dark. Most of the time I'm afraid to walk out to my car anyway, it's so black out there. You guys can hide in the museum, in back of the old hanger, and near the deserted motel. You can spread out. I can't see anything that would go wrong."

"Out of the mouth of babes," Ben got up and hugged Cynthia, smirking behind her back at Adam. "That's perfect. Let's do it."

The meeting was over five minutes later. Cynthia said she would make the call at nine o'clock the next morning and set the meeting for ten o'clock that night.

Everybody had one more beer before the gathering broke up. Just as he was leaving, Joe turned to Adam and said, "Pray for me, Big Brother. I sat here through the meeting knowing something is going to happen tonight. I think I'm going to see your crazy lady first hand."

As Adam was walking out the door, the last of the brothers to leave, Cynthia was back at his side. "And now, if you'll come with me to my new apartment, I'm going to show you what a really crazy woman acts like."

CHAPTER TWENTY

JOE FIGURED HE'D DRIVEN THE ROAD FROM SIDNEY TO THE farm almost one thousand times. The number had to be that high when you counted shopping trips with his parents and brothers, dates to the movies and dances when he was in high school, and hanging out drinking beer with college friends. But he had never driven the route so slowly before. Though determined to spend the night at the farm, he kept hoping the car would magically turn on its own and go to Jake's house. He would rather stay anywhere than the house his grandfather had built. He also would never be able to live with himself if he chickened-out.

As did the rest of the family, Joe had always discounted Adam's fears of the place. His family had lived there since his grandfather built it, and he hadn't included any special rooms for spirits from the beyond. Adam's ghosts had always been his problem. Nobody else had ever seen them.

Tonight, however, everything seemed different. Joe's skepticism and cynicism were missing in action, replaced by a gnawing suspicion that spirits really did exist. Once he'd opened his mind to that possibility, his bravado had also disappeared; it was one thing to believe in ghosts, but it was another to meet one.

All too soon he was in the yard, his hand automatically turning off the engine and removing the key. His mind considered driving to Texas.

As though in a mental fog and incapable of decision-making, commanded by post-hypnotic suggestions to act against his will, he walked through the back door of the old house and into the kitchen. Joe didn't have his older brother's experience in coping with such fears. He didn't turn on the radio to fill the void, and he wouldn't talk out loud, afraid it would signal he was cracking up. He didn't carry a weapon. He couldn't imagine it doing any good.

His heart thumping against his ribs, he sat in the kitchen believing a crazy woman with a big knife was going to hack him into bits before the sun came up in the morning. Just as the family must who refuses to keep guns in the house and confronts armed intruders, Joe faced his mortality.

Waiting for death, or at least an encounter with the dead, Joe hoped his fears were merely the power of suggestion. Adam had talked about his dammed ghosts for forty years. Combining his brother's stories with the two bodies dug up in the yard gave Joe every reason to be susceptible to rampant imagination. He was reacting to stress and tension - nothing more, nothing less. He might have been able to convince himself it was all psychological, if only it hadn't been so dammed quiet. The silence seemed magnified and chilled, as though he were deep in an underground tomb listening for the sounds of the dead.

'Unworldly! That's what it is,' he thought, 'unworldly.' He'd been alone in the house many times. He liked being alone. He knew how it sounded when he was alone, and being alone had never sounded as this did before. 'The house is too quiet and too unworldly. I'm alone with death. No, it *isn't death. I'm alone with evil, an evil that has killed before and is now stalking me.'*

Joe stared through the doorway to the rest of the house waiting for evil to appear for so long he grew cold and stiff. Glancing up at the clock on the kitchen wall, he used the Lord's name in vain and instantly regretted it. He was beginning to believe there might be an accounting of his sins at the Pearly Gates much sooner than he'd ever expected.

The ornate timepiece, a gift his father had given his mother, showed he'd been inside for less than fifteen minutes. He knew that couldn't be right. He'd been there most of the night. Then he checked his wristwatch and was horrified to discover it agreed with the clock.

In his personal Twilight Zone, where minutes passed as hours, Joe thought about running out to his car and driving away. Nobody would ever know. He could stay in a nice motel and tell everyone he'd spent the night in the house alone. He could even truthfully say he hadn't seen anything supernatural. His brothers would believe him and laugh at Adam. Adam was the weird one. Joe could stay anywhere else, and it would be fine. He had changed since his drive out to the farm from town. He could chicken out now and still be able to live with himself.

He would have, except he had always prided himself on having a rational and logical mind. Adam was an academic and a dreamer, Jake was too damned cynical for his own good, and Ben was a wounded war hero who didn't want anything to break his routine. Joe was the enlightened one, the engineer who held empiricism and the scientific method in highest regard. Leaving and giving in to his fears would be denying himself. If he ran, he would no longer be the man he believed he was.

Joe finally decided he would do the same as any other red-blooded American would under those circumstances; he'd chug half of a bottle of vodka and pass out. If he awoke long enough to see any ghosts, he would finish off the bottle and be too drunk to open his eyes again until the next afternoon.

The vodka ran down his throat as water had when he'd worked in the hayfields as a kid. Slamming the bottle down on his mother's kitchen table, Joe started towards the downstairs bedroom, alcohol igniting a fire in his stomach. "Downstairs, hell," he bellowed loud enough to wake the dead. "Adam can sleep downstairs. I'm going to spend the night in the haunted room. That will show them who the brave one is."

Undressing to his boxers in the room with the built-in closet, alcohol's courage enveloped Joe. He was no longer aware of a sense of malevolence, nor was he nervously expecting visits from a crazy woman. 'Depend on the Goose and Sleep Safely. That should be an advertising slogan for a brand of vodka,' he thought as he closed his eyes. There had never been anything in the house to be afraid of, except Adam's nightmares.

But Joe couldn't sleep. He had forgotten something between the fears, the vodka, and pouring himself into bed. He had something important to do. The camera! That was it! He had forgotten to set the motion-activated camera in the dining room to operate. He would not be able to sleep until it was ready. A blank tape would be the proof he needed to convince Adam there was no reason to be afraid.

The moonlight was so bright he didn't need to turn on any lights. Halfway down the stairs, at the exact spot he had always hit his head when he descended too fast as a kid, he heard the camera turn on. The faint click magnified by the silence of the house startled Joe. He jumped straight up in panic and hit his head. Frozen on the steps, bleeding from a small head wound, he believed the woman with a knife was in the dining room waiting for him.

The vodka he had gulped to dim his senses was now working in reverse. He had never felt so terrified and anxious. To make it worse, he felt as if he was about to vomit, the vile taste already invading the back of his mouth. Joe once again decided he would do what any red-blooded American in a haunted house with a manifestation occurring and a belly full of booze that wasn't going to stay down would do. He closed his eyes, ran out the front door, and expelled the remains of his chicken dinner and expensive vodka all over his mother's evergreens.

Minutes later, he walked back into the house past the no-longer running camera and into his parent's bedroom. Sober and sick to his stomach, he didn't care if every ghost in western Nebraska frolicked around the house without their sheets on as long as they left him alone. He was in the sanctuary of his mother's bed. If he couldn't curl up with her for protection, cuddling her pillows in the bed she'd slept in for fifty years was next best.

His eyes clenched shut and blankets tucked under his chin, Joe thought of his mother and fell asleep, a sense of peace pervading the house that only moments before had seemed filled with evil. The electronic sound of the camera turning on again less than twenty feet from where he slept, reverberated through the room, but Joe didn't hear it. He was dreaming of when he was young and his mother had been the most important person in his life.

His family was at the lake, in his dream he was playing in the sand with his brothers on one of those rare days when the fields were too wet to cultivate. His mother, wearing a yellow sundress, was bending over to give him a plate of fried chicken, his favorite food. He looked up, squinting into the sun to take the chicken and smile at her when his dream morphed into a nightmare.

Instead of his mother, a strangely dressed young man and woman were standing over him. Instead of a plate full of chicken, the male was holding a large knife out to him in a manner reminiscent of a medieval vassal presenting a sword to his master. Instead of being at the lake, he was in the bedroom of his parent's house.

Joe stared at them without blinking or looking away, convinced he was only dreaming. He studied every detail of their appearance until they disappeared backward through the wall. The gentle click of the camera in the living room either turning on or off (he didn't know which) awakened him. He was sorry the dream ended, believing he had seen the murdered young people as they had appeared in life, pulled into vision by his imagination. Snuggling deeper into the blankets, he smiled warmly and began to fall asleep again, hoping the couple would return. Maybe they would even bring his grandmother with them.

Abruptly, he sat upright, the rational portion of his brain disrupting his feeling of contentment. It had to be just a coincidence the camera came on just as they disappeared through the wall into the dining room. Hadn't it? It had been only a dream, and dreams can't cause electronic equipment to run. Of course not!

Joe wanted to believe it had only been a dream. The film would prove what it had been, wouldn't it? He wanted to see the film, and he wanted to run out of the house, climb into his car, and drive away. For some reason he couldn't explain, even to himself, all he could do was lie in his mother's bed.

Slowly Joe began to fall asleep again, thinking of his mother and of being in that room with her. He had loved rising early as a child, running down the stairs, climbing into bed between his parents, and waking up his father who would then rouse his older brothers for their morning chores. Joe would lie in bed with his mother, feeling incredibly loved, and fall back to sleep. Later, on cold winter mornings, she would stand over him holding out a cup of cocoa, the wonderful chocolate smell calling him from his slumber.

Mimicking the actions in his memories, Joe slowly opened his eyes to see her, screamed, and rolled to the other side of the bed in terror. Instead of his mother, the woman from Adam's nightmares was standing over him holding a long-bladed knife. Instead of his mother's freshly made-up face, the features he stared into dripped blood.

To Joe's horror, the specter didn't disappear at the sound of his screams as they always did in the movies. Instead, she slowly reached out in the same gesture the young male spirit had done and offered him the weapon. Suddenly, she dropped the wicked blade and turned to face the wall separating the bedroom from the dining room, holding out her arms in a welcoming gesture.

Joe stared in fascination as the two young people reappeared; this time they were smiling and holding hands. Floating effortlessly, they moved to the woman's side and embraced her.

A great sense of peace swept across the room as the three translucent visitors smiled down at him. As they began fading, Joe recognized his grandmother as the woman who had been holding the knife and felt her love wash over him. In that moment, he knew two truths: ghosts were real and his grandmother had not been the horror of Adam's nightmares. She had not been the murderer.

Again, the sound of the camera clicking on startled him. The alarm clock read 2 a.m., two hours since he'd climbed back into bed after his original visit by the young couple. But that couldn't be. Their second appearance, when they'd joined his grandmother, had lasted for only several minutes at the most. Two hours? What happened to the rest of the time?

He hadn't been asleep when he seen his grandmother. He had just been lying in bed awake, daydreaming in the middle of the night. Hadn't he? He didn't remember going to sleep, but he must have. Again, his inherent logical and rational mind-set provided the answer.

Joe realized he must have fallen back to sleep after his first dream. The second visitation had been just another dream. He had wanted so much to believe he had seen his grandmother and felt her love, something he had never known because she'd died two years before his birth. Accepting that it had all been a subconscious product of his wishes was difficult. But what else could he do? No other rational explanation existed.

With his mind whirling over the facts, Joe recalled Adam mentioning a folder on the refrigerator containing a picture of their grandmother and Consuelo. He suddenly had an urge to see what the young Mexican woman looked like.

He walked through the house without turning on the lights, remembering the way from his childhood, even reaching up and taking the folder off the refrigerator in the dark. After turning on a light, he sat at the table and waited several moments for his eyes to adjust to the light. Joe struggled to bring Consuelo's features from the dream to the fore of his consciousness.

Three pictures were in the folder. The first was of his grandmother, and once again he saw how beautiful she had been, the faded photograph softening and accentuating her beauty. The second was of a young cowboy holding a rope with a six-gun holstered around his waist standing next to a rifle leaning against a bale of hay. The inscription on the back identifying the cowboy wearing sheepskin chaps as his grandfather was still a shock, although Adam had told them all about their grandfather's secret past.

Joe wanted to take the time to close his eyes and imagine his grandfather as the dashing young man in the picture, but he couldn't put off looking at the third photograph. He needed to see Consuelo while he still remembered how she'd looked in his dream.

The picture was of two young women. His eyes lit first on his grandmother and he smiled. When his gaze fastened on the smiling, beautiful young woman with a Spanish-style comb in her hair, his hands began shaking so violently he had to lay the picture on the table and study every detail.

"It's her. Good God!" he yelled, laughing and crying with joy. "The girl in the picture is the girl in my dream. They look just alike - it's her! And the boy, the boy . . ." he stuttered realizing what he'd seen. "The boy looks just like her, as if they were freaking twins!"

His mind racing, Joe began searching for a way to explain such a bizarre coincidence. He might have seen the picture before. Had he looked at it last night and forgotten? Maybe he'd looked at it after he drank the vodka, and he'd been too drunk to remember. No, that wasn't it. He hadn't had that much to drink, and he had never seen the picture before.

Joe could consider only two possibilities. Either ghosts were able to reveal themselves in dreams, making you believe their manifestations were dreams, or he had seen the picture long ago as a child. At three o'clock in the morning, his mind still a fog of 'what if', and 'how could that be,' Joe went back to bed.

Fifteen minutes later, Adam's crazy woman with the weird hat and the huge knife rushed out of the closet directly at him. Brandishing the knife above her head and screaming, she was obviously intent on killing him. Joe knew exactly what time it was because as soon as she ran past him and disappeared into the wall, he rolled over and looked at the clock. This time he simply didn't know if he'd been awake or asleep, and he didn't care. Whoever the last woman had once been, he'd gotten a good enough look to know he had never seen her before. She hadn't been his grandmother.

The night had been too much for Joe and trying to separate reality from dreams too taxing. Unlike Adam who'd battled the dilemma for years, Joe chose not to suffer. He accepted the answer on faith alone, a new experience in his empirically based existence. His grandmother had been innocent, and she'd made sure he knew the truth.

He'd had enough. He couldn't sleep, so he decided to sit up the rest of the night and wait for the sun. He grabbed a dog-eared paperback novel from a shelf. After turning on every light in the house, he began reading. Before he knew it, sunlight was pouring through the windows. Just as he finished the book, a fast-moving, tan pickup truck fishtailed across the graveled driveway and slammed to a stop by the back door.

CHAPTER TWENTY-ONE

WILBUR ROBERTS HADN'T BEEN SLEEPING WELL. HE WAS doing his great uncle's dirty work for the money, not because he'd ever felt any loyalty to the old man. He enjoyed sticking it to those assholes, but Autie's game was getting old. Besides, as far as he could figure, there was nothing in it for him.

The old man had just wanted that Adam guy run off with his tail dragging between his legs. At first Wilbur thought it would be easy, but after shooting at him, knocking him out, destroying his car, and running his woman off the road, the guy had called in reinforcements.

That's great, bring 'em on, the game would be more fun, but it was time they started playing it his way. Somebody was going to get hurt, and he was going to do the hurting. But before anything else happened, he was going to give that bitch what she had coming to her.

He'd sat up in his trailer most of the night after making sure she was staying at the motel again. Stuck-up bitch, always acting too good for him whenever he'd tried to talk to her. Now she was screwing that jerk-wad. Why else would she be staying at the motel?

It wasn't fair, and it wasn't right. He'd tried being nice to her more than once, and she hadn't bothered to give him the time of day. All this Adam guy had to do was drive into town, and she'd jumped in the sack with him. Well, she was about to get what was coming to her. Stupid old Autie, his dim-witted brother, Earl, and everybody else could go to hell. Take what you want. That's a man's way. That's what his old man had beaten into him with his fists, and that's what he was going to do.

He knew she usually left for the museum about seven in the morning. All he had to do was wait for her in the motel parking lot when she went to her car, grab her, and drive away. He could do it so nobody would notice. She would pay for humiliating him. Humiliating him by screwing that dip-shit and rejecting him. Snatching the snatch, that's what he was going to do. The idea made him laugh so much, he'd stayed up all-night watching television, smoking dope, and getting ready.

By six forty-five in the morning, he'd parked his tan pickup on the other side of a grain truck from her car. Some dumb-ass farmer came to town in his truck, got drunk, and couldn't drive home. This would make the snatch easy. He'd sneak up behind her as she unlocked her car, drag her around the truck, and throw her into the cage in the back of his pickup.

His homemade cage, snatch jail he called it, was his best idea ever. Made to resemble the toolboxes most farmers and ranchers had in the back of their trucks, his had small air holes for breathing. She wouldn't be screaming as he drove out of town. The ether-soaked handkerchief he'd hold over her face would knock her out. She could wake up within three minutes of the snatch and scream all she wanted. Nobody would hear ever her again but him, and he enjoyed those sounds.

———

Driving towards Medicine Lodge on the Interstate, Wilbur laughed at how easy it had been. Went just like his plan. She'd never known he was behind her until he was holding the ether over her nose, and then it had been too late. She'd gone out like a light, and he'd dumped her in the cage without anyone seeing.

His luck was finally changing. He'd always had miserable luck, no matter how hard he worked or planned, something always went wrong. It had only been bad luck the dumb bitch in Wyoming had escaped from his trailer. It wouldn't have happened to anyone else. With better luck, he'd have kept her captive for as long as he wanted, done whatever he'd wanted with her, and then dumped her dead in the desert or the mountains. He'd had it all planned out, it was just bad luck she got away.

This was different. Good luck made him strong. He was in control and nothing could go wrong. He could do anything he wanted with this one and then bury her in the middle of a cornfield where nobody would ever find her. Anybody who tried to get in his way would regret it.

The irony of it all was righteous. He was going to do her in that old house. The one where he and his family could never go as kids, where their side of the family had to leave for no fault of their own, and where that jerk-wad had dug up the bones.

He didn't know how the skeletons that bugged Autie so much had died, but he knew how the stuck-up whore in the back was going to go. He would strangle her while he was doing her. Thinking about it made him higher than shooting crack. That's why he had to twist the steering wheel and turn into the yard so fast, fishtailing and throwing gravel as he fought to control the truck. He'd been thinking so much about the pleasure the woman was going to give him, he'd almost missed the driveway.

Recognizing the truck as the one that had forced Cynthia off the road, Joe ran to the door to meet his relative. Looking around frantically for a weapon, he remembered with dismay Adam had taken the 20-gauge Jake kept on the porch to shoot skunks. Focused on the man leaping out of the pickup, Joe stumbled over the crumbling concrete of the step, landing on the hardpan dirt, wincing as sharp pain tore through his right leg.

He had to get up, shrug off the injury to his leg, and help Cynthia. As he was falling, the man had pulled her over the side of the truck by her hair and slammed her viciously to the ground. She could be hurt. Ignoring the searing pain, Joe pulled himself up, using the fence for support. The barrel of a pistol jammed into the side of his head announced he was too slow. The first time he heard his mystery relative speak, the voice wasn't friendly.

"Well, looky here! I suppose you be one of my shit-bird cousins. I didn't think any of you would still be out here. Now that you are, maybe you want to join the fun. Huh, what do you say about that? Want some of this fine looking woman?"

Joe saw the terror in Cynthia's eyes. He would do anything to protect her. He would tell the animal to let her go, that she had nothing to do with it. The man could do anything he wanted with him. This problem was between their families. Maybe he could even appeal to the guy, after all, the same blood ran through their veins, surely they could work this out peacefully. But he never had a chance. Swimming through the torrents of pain tearing into his leg, trying to find the right words, he heard the voice of his cousin again.

"Aw hell! You're just in the way, and there won't be any left for you anyhow."

"What, what're you talking about?" Joe stammered just before his world exploded into a violent light that abruptly turned black. Unconscious before he started falling, Joe's weight centered on the injured leg. The jagged ends of his broken tibia and fibula pierced the skin above his ankle.

Seeing the blood pooling under Joe's leg, Cynthia fell to her knees. She began rolling up his pant leg to expose the injury when Wilbur started pulling her toward the house by her hair. "Come on bitch. He was just a little interruption to our party," he growled, pointing the gun directly into her face. "I'll get you comfortable inside and then take care of him."

"Please, wait," she screamed, her voice straining from fear and pain. "He broke his leg. Let me bandage and splint it, then I'll do anything you want. Please let me go. I have to help him."

She had decided in the cage she wasn't going to die. And she wasn't going to let Joe die either. She would play along with this guy's sick games until they could escape.

Wilbur pulled her into the house, not speaking again until he'd thrown her into a chair and started tying her hands and feet to its arms and legs. "No reason to help him. He's going to die and so are you. How long you stay alive depends on how nice you are."

"Just wait a minute," Cynthia pleaded. "Nobody has to die. I'll do what you want. We can party. Then you can let us go. You can have your fun and get away with it. Why risk going to jail? I promise neither of us will say anything."

The expression on her captor's face broke through Cynthia's resolve. If the devil's minions walked the earth inflicting harm on God's creatures, she knew she was staring into the eyes of his most vicious disciple. Every story she had ever read about psychopaths and serial killers described their dead eyes, comparing them to the black orbs of sharks circling prey. But his eyes were not dead, they were pure evil. Cynthia felt as if she were a Christian staring into the eyes of a Roman lion.

"That's right. Neither you nor he is going to say anything. He's about to die and the only thing keeping you alive is how I can use you." After tying one of the cloth napkins he had taken from a bureau in the room around her mouth, Wilbur licked her face before backhanding her. "Now just keep quiet, and keep your pants on till I get back. Then we'll play. Get it? Keep your pants on! That's a pretty good joke."

After he walked out the door, Cynthia strained against the ropes, hoping she could tip the chair over and shuffle out to the kitchen where she would find a knife to cut herself free. Unfortunately, her will to survive was not enough to force her to tear her eyes away from the macabre scene outside the picture window.

The man was smiling as he bound Joe's hands behind him, and then tied his legs together, jerking the broken one savagely. After stuffing a rag into Joe's mouth, Wilbur yanked him over to the ruins of the storm cellar where Adam had found the skeletons. With one section of steel plating still in place, it took him only a few minutes to roll Joe under the metal and pile stones and dirt along the sides, burying his captive alive. When he finished, he started laughing and yelling loud enough for Cynthia to hear.

"There. That'll do you. I'll bet it gets so hot in there it'll fry your brains and eyeballs afore you're dead. I'd like to stay around and hear you sizzle, but I've got a pretty lady to attend to."

Again, Cynthia decided her only chance was to reason with the monster. There had to be some trace of humanity inside him. She had to get through to him. As he pulled off her gag, she pleaded, "Now, please. I know your name is Wilbur. You're Adam's cousin. I know everything about you and your family. I know you've been arrested for rape before, and that's probably what's scaring you. Listen to me, we can work this out without anybody getting killed or going to jail. "Wait. Don't . . ."

Cynthia swam back to consciousness after the monster had hit her in the face with his fist, emerging from pain-free darkness into hell. The pig had her clothes off and was lying next to her masturbating, grunting and slobbering, his hate-filled eyes closed, lost in the pleasure psychopaths take in the terror of their victims. He had tied her arms and legs to a bed's four corners.

Vulnerable and unable to move except to twist her body, she lie quietly and recalled stories of how victims often left their bodies, enduring hideous treatment by sending their minds to pleasant places. Cynthia tried turning off her physical being but was about to abandon the attempt, convinced the stories were myths, when she felt a soft hand tenderly caress her stomach as another gently rubbed her cheek. It was exactly what her mother had done when she'd hurt herself as a little girl. The room had grown quiet, and she could no longer hear the ogre lying beside her. She opened her eyes and saw Adam's grandmother standing beside her.

Consuelo and Jesus, dressed in Victorian era finery, stood on each side of Sarah. Cynthia felt total peace in the love shining down from their faces. They were there to help her endure her suffering. They were with her. Their love would lift her above the pain a mere mortal could inflict.

It was as if the monster was there, but he wasn't. She was alone with the three spirits. Cynthia would never forget the warmth and love in Sarah's voice.

"It will be all right, dear. Soon you will be free. My family is coming for you. My dear George tried to help me long ago, but he couldn't because he didn't know how evil others could be. My grandsons are coming to help us. They love you, and we love you."

Grateful, reassured by their love, Cynthia wanted to make sure the spirits understood that Joe was already dying. "Sarah. Can't you help me now? Please. I must go to your grandson, Joe. He's buried him outside. Please help me."

"I cannot dear, and we cannot stay. Help is coming, and you and Joe will be safe. My family will soon be here. They will free us. Our terrible nightmare is almost over. You must be as brave as poor Consuelo and Jesus have been.

"Soon we will be able to join the rest of our loved ones. I know my poor George misses me so. Good-bye. Remember your soul is always free. Be brave. My family is finally coming to help us."

"Please don't go. Please stay. I need you. Help me," Cynthia begged, but it was no use. The spirits began floating backward into the wall behind them. Once again she was alone with the monster, and now he was standing over her, his fist drawn back to strike her again.

"Who you talking to, bitch?" he asked, his voice sounding to her as if he hissed the words through the poisonous fangs of a prairie rattler. "Who do you think is going to help you? Ain't anybody coming to help you? Now I'm gonna untie you, and you're gonna go make me some breakfast and not try to get away. You understand?"

She had to do as the monster wanted. She had to stay alive. Adam and his brothers were coming. "Don't hit me again. I'll get it. I won't try to run away. Untie me and let me up."

"That's smart of you, gal," Wilbur said, sounding pleased with his victim's submission. "You get busy, but remember, try to get away and I'll not only kill you, I'll get your boyfriend out there and start skinning him like a rabbit. You act nice, and maybe I'll let him live for a while. You don't, and both of you will die wishing your momma never met your daddy."

Cynthia found eggs, bacon, and even bread for toast. As she was frying a regular country breakfast for the monster, she watched him grab the bottle of vodka and sit on the steel plating above Joe's tomb. Every time he took a drink, he kicked the metal as if he intended to make sure the man buried below stayed awake.

CHAPTER TWENTY-TWO

ADAM FIGURED HE WAS TOO OLD TO HAVE AN AFFAIR, BUT he wouldn't have missed this one for the world. Once he was home, he would have to work through the relationship. It had taken on more importance than he had ever thought it would.

Maybe he had been susceptible because something was missing in his marriage, maybe because something was missing in him, or maybe he had always been a wild and crazy kind of guy. Whatever - he'd work on it later. Right now, he didn't have time for a hypothetical Freudian couch.

Strong coffee and a good breakfast would clear the cobwebs after a hot tub eased his aches and pains. He needed to be alert when he joined Cynthia in the museum for her call to Autie. If the old man agreed to meet her and everything went as planned, Adam would finally discover what had happened in the storm cellar more than eighty years ago. He would finally learn the story behind his nightmares.

His cell phone began playing the Brandenburg Concerto just as he was leaving for the café. He assumed it would be Cynthia asking if he was up yet, probably employing a double entendre to wish him good morning.

"Hello," he answered grumpily, she would know he was only being dramatic.

"Why hello yourself, you grouchy old fart," Jake retorted. "What's the matter? Not enough sleep, or did you get too much?"

Adam considered telling him people with a Boulder lifestyle didn't ever get up before noon, but Jake would have believed him, the sarcasm passing way over his head. "Oh, its nothing. Just a little tired, I suppose. What's up? I'm sure you aren't calling just to inquire about my well-being."

Pleasantries exchanged, such as they were, Jake was back to being himself. "Well, I don't know what's going on. You sure your friend from the museum didn't decide to sell us out and go ahead and make a deal with Autie?"

"Come on Jake, you can do better than that," Adam said, clearly impatient. "What's with you? I'm meeting her in an hour to make the call. Why don't you drop this tough guy act?"

"Might be because Ben and I have been trying to call Joe for an hour and he doesn't answer. We drove out here to the farm and the tan pickup is parked in the driveway. Only thing I can think of is she set the meeting ahead when we wouldn't know."

"Jake. What about Joe? He's supposed to be out there. Didn't you see him?" He wouldn't sell us out - and neither would Cynthia. Something else is going on."

Adam could hear him discuss Joe's role with Ben in the background. When Jake got back on the phone, worry tinged his voice. "I believe you. She's not selling out. But then where's Joe? What's happened to him? He wouldn't meet with those guys without us."

"I don't know," Adam replied, failing to think of a reasonable explanation. "We've got to get on top of this.

Wilbur and Earl are violent men. We need to make sure Joe's all right." Running through the exigencies as quickly as he could, a multi-step plan began to form in his mind.

"Jake. You and Ben get somewhere you can watch the place without being seen. I'll call Cynthia and see if she knows anything. I'll get back to you in ten."

The museum's phone rang more than fifteen times before a recording of Cynthia's voice told Adam to call back during business hours. After waiting five minutes, he tried again with the same result. Maybe she'd gone for coffee or supplies. Somebody was going to have to check.

Jake answered his cell on the third ring. "That you, Adam? We're parked behind the barn where we can watch the house. Nothing's going on that we can see. What did Cynthia say? She know anything about Joe?"

"There's no answer at the museum Jake, and that's strange. One of you needs to stay there and watch the house since you're a lot closer than I am, and the other has to go find her. You both have phones?"

"Yeah, Ben and I each have one. I'll crawl up into the loft and watch the place. I'll send Ben right away. He'll call me in fifteen, and I'll get back to you."

As Adam said good-bye, urging them to hurry, he couldn't help but think something was terribly wrong. He hadn't wanted to worry Jake and Ben anymore than necessary, but this didn't seem like either Cynthia or Joe.

Adam sat on the bed waiting. The time it took Ben to drive to Medicine Lodge was going to seem like an eternity. His fidgeting was almost out of control when a knock broke the silence. Before he got to the door, Cynthia's friend, Sue, the owner of the motel, breezed into the room carrying a pot of coffee and two cups. She was laughing as she enjoyed her little joke.

"Hi, Adam," she said, placing the pot and cups on the dresser. "You'd better rouse Cynthia, she's late for work. Here's some coffee to make it easier." Seeing the bed empty and the bathroom door open threw her off for a second. "Oh, I see she just left. Wonder how I missed her in the hall? You two must have had quite a morning."

"I don't know what you're talking about." he said. "You know she leaves before seven. She's been gone for over an hour."

Sue's smile changed to an expression of concern. "But, but, that's not possible," she stammered. "Her car is out in the lot. At least, it was when I left the lobby with this coffee. Don't tease me! Where is she?"

"I'm telling you the truth," he told her. "She left her apartment an hour and a half ago. I'm supposed to meet her in the museum in less than an hour. . . ."

The concerto interrupted his explanation, and he quickly picked up the phone. Ben was yelling before Adam could say hello. "Hey, Big Brother. I don't know what the deal is, but she isn't here and hasn't been. I talked to a gardener waiting out in front, and he said he hadn't seen her. He needs to talk to her, and he's looked all over town. She hasn't been around here."

Adam told him to get back to the farm as fast as possible. He had just started telling Sue his brothers were looking for Cynthia when the Brandenburg Concerto played with urgency the composer never imagined, sounding far more like the shrill ringing of a 1950's party line telephone than an elegant orchestral arrangement.

"This is Jake," his older brother whispered over the phone. "Shut up and listen. Wilbur just came out of the house and is sitting on that steel over the old shelter, drinking booze, kicking the steel, and yelling. I think he's got Joe under there and. . .Oh Shit! Cynthia just came out of the house bringing him a plate. Her nose is bleeding, and she's not wearing a shirt and . . . Oh Christ! He just grabbed her hair and pulled her to the ground. Now he's kicked her and is pointing a gun at her. I've got to . . ."

"Wait. Wait, Jake. You've got to stay where you are," Adam told him, struggling to remain calm. "You're just going to get killed if you go running down there. Hold on! I'll call Ben. I'll be back in two."

Ben answered on the first ring. Adam passed Jake's news to him and told him to turn around and collect a couple of rifles and ammunition. Ben still had plenty of hunting buddies in town who wouldn't think anything of it if he said he and his brothers were going coyote hunting and needed to borrow weapons. "You get in the loft with Jake. If Wilbur is still outside, take him out if it looks like he's going to kill Cynthia, but don't shoot unless it's absolutely necessary. Hurry!"

The thought of calling the police as Adam would have done automatically in Boulder crossed his mind, but he decided against it immediately. The only officers available would be a few small town deputies, and it would take forty-five minutes to an hour for them to get there. And what were they going to do when they did? Probably drive into the yard with flashing lights and blaring sirens, alerting Wilbur so he'd have time to kill his captives and get ready for a shootout.

Cynthia and Joe's only chances, if their captor wouldn't give himself up, depended on taking Wilbur out with one shot. Ben was the best shot Adam had ever seen. He should be. That's all he ever did except play a little golf with Jake and go fishing. He'd made his reputation as a sniper in the jungles of Southeast Asia, and if he decided it was time for Wilbur to die, their cousin would never know what hit him.

Adam and his brothers were also in the best position to talk Wilbur into giving up. Negotiating with the police meant jail if he surrendered. The man's own relation might be able to convince him a stay in the lock-up wasn't the only option. This was still a family matter, and relatives could resolve it best.

Sue was still standing there, looking as if she'd just heard Russian missiles were passing over the ice cap. She'd learned enough from the phone conservations to know Cynthia's disappearance had turned into a life and death matter. Adam sat her in a chair, told her to take a deep breath, and related exactly what was going on out at his family's old farm.

Her hands flew to her mouth, fear for her friend recorded in her terror-stricken look. Adam was sure she was going to either scream or hyperventilate, and he didn't need the cops or the paramedics rushing into the room. In the movies, somebody would have slapped her and she would have thanked them because she needed it. Adam pulled her hands from her face and none-to-gently shook her shoulders.

"Stop it. Calm down. If you want to help Cynthia, you need to do exactly as I tell you. My brothers and I are her only chance. Has she told you what's going on? Not about her and me, but about the bodies and my family."

Stiffening her back and wiping tears away with her palms, Sue composed herself. "Yes. I know most of it. I know someone forced her off the road and you've been shot at and beat-up. She thinks your one-hundred-year-old uncle from Oklahoma is behind it."

Adam quickly filled her in on the rest of the story and then laid out his plans, such as they were. "My brothers are crack shots, best I know. They're already in place," he was stretching the truth a little, hoping it would calm her, "and they're sighted in on Wilbur's head. If he tries anything, he's a dead man. The cops can only confuse the situation and put Cynthia's life in danger. Do you understand?"

Bending forward, sliding her chair closer, Sue spoke in hushed tones. "You're absolutely right about the police. I know most of our local boys in blue. They're pretty good at handling the occasional bar fight, but a shoot-out would be out of their league. You'd have to call in the highway patrol and that would take too long. Why don't they just shoot the son-of a-bitch and have it over with?"

"Because I want to try to resolve this without anybody getting killed. My family has suffered for too long. For sure Autie has. I'm going to go get him, Earl, and their mother by force if I have to, and have them talk Wilbur into giving himself up."

She was ready to go before he finished speaking. "Great idea! I'll drive my Bronco. It's big and has a lot of room. Cynthia is going to need me." Rushing to the door, she hollered back over her shoulder, "Are you coming or not?"

She drove up to Earl's house, a post World War II bungalow that couldn't have enclosed more than seven hundred square feet surrounded by a lawn that looked as if water hadn't touched it since the war ended. Sitting in a chair on the sidewalk as if he had been expecting company was the oldest man Adam had ever seen. As Sue slammed to a stop, Adam's great-uncle, surprisingly nimble for his age, stood up and pushed the chair away. Standing straight with both hands on his cane, he struck a pose much more as if he was a distinguished diplomat than a crazed murderer.

Age had not diminished the power of his voice. "Boy! You must be Adam. I was hoping you'd be coming. I know what he's done and where he is, he called us on the phone. Sounds like he's plumb gone nuts.

"I reckon this has gone on long enough. It's time to end the fight. Let's go get my boy and thet girl. Earl and his momma already lit out. Don't know where they're going and don't care. They don't want no part of this. Now help me into the car. I've got to save my boy! He's the only one I've cared about in a long time."

Sue knew a way out of town where she didn't have to stop for any lights or traffic. Once she hit the highway, her speedometer pegged out at the maximum it would register. Autie held a death grip on the dash next to her in the front seat while Adam urged her to go faster. They were halfway to the farm when the concerto began playing again.

"Adam, you won't believe this," Jake screamed into the phone. "Wilbur had gone back inside and Ben worked his way around to the side of the house, trying to see through the picture window. Anyway, just as he got into position, Wilbur came tearing down from the upstairs, ran to his car, fell on his ass twice getting through the gate, and drove away scattering gravel over a country mile.

"Ben ran inside and found Cynthia. She's bruised but fine. Joe's alive. He's under the steel. I've got to get him out."

The phone went dead before Adam could react. He was still telling Sue and Autie the news when they crested a hill and spotted the tan pickup in the ditch. Wilbur was outside the cab, leaning over the hood. Adam ran to him holding the 20-gauge at the ready, prepared to blow Wilbur to hell in front of their great-uncle, the only living soul on earth who loved him. As Adam reached him, his cousin threw his arms over his head and fell to the ground sobbing.

CHAPTER TWENTY-THREE

ADAM BAILED OUT OF THE MOVING SUV AS SUE TURNED into the driveway. Cynthia was in his arms before he was halfway up the crumbling sidewalk. "Oh my God! I'm sorry. I'm so sorry I got you mixed up in this," he murmured, lifting her head so he could see how serious her injuries were. He was ready to apologize again when she smiled through swollen lips, both eyes beginning to discolor.

"Don't say that," she whispered, placing a finger over his lips. "Don't ever. I don't think it had anything to do with you. I've been ducking that bastard for years. I just didn't know he was your relative, the one you were talking about."

Adam thought they should pull away from each other since his brothers and her friend were standing around them grinning - only Jake looked away embarrassed, acting overly concerned for Autie's ability to wait in the sun. As Adam was deciding he didn't care what anyone thought, Ben and Sue joined them in the hug. Autie waited, staring into the house through the open front door as if he were peering into a shrine.

Blood still seeped into Joe's hair through the bandage of cotton and ripped sheets Ben had fashioned. He was lying in the shade of the house, his leg splinted with a traction splint Ben had learned how to make during the war. Cynthia rewarded his pain-weakened howdy with a hug after she broke away from his brothers.

"Damn, girl, I thought we were dead," he told her. "I was so worried about you. But I couldn't move. I can tell you one thing. I'm never sticking my head underground again."

"You are my hero, Joe," she said and kissed him on the lips. "You came running out to rescue me. You should have run the other way as fast as you could."

Joe looked away sheepishly. "I know you're right. I should have used better sense. I would have been able to save us both, if I had. But I didn't. I was so sure he was going to kill you, I just ran out and hoped for the best."

Jake walked over to the door, holding it open for Autie, and called to his brothers and Cynthia. Instead of cynical, his voice sounded warm and good-natured. "Well, all of you heroes and heroines can stand out here in the sun if you want. Autie and I are going to have a beer and celebrate everyone's safety. First though, we need to find the door lover boy there took off the hinges so we can cart Joe into the house."

"Wilbur! Don't forget him! Somebody please help my boy!" Autie pleaded from inside the house, his voice breaking with strain. "You've got to help him."

In Adam's joy at seeing Cynthia and Joe alive, he had forgotten he'd tied their tormentor in a collection of knots that would have made Houdini pale. "Don't worry. I'll get him," Ben said. "Adam and Jake can carry Joe. I'll fix Mr. Wilbur up so he's warm and comfy."

After carrying Joe into the house and making him comfortable in their father's old recliner, Adam walked outside to be alone with Cynthia, stealing any moment available. "I was so worried. Are you all right? Did he? Uh, do I need to take you to the hospital?"

Cynthia kissed him passionately and for what seemed an eternity, but when she pulled away, he knew her Great Affair was over. "No. He didn't. I'm fine, just a little bruised is all. Boy, are you going to have some stories to tell your wife and kids. I'm going to gather my children and grand-children around me for the next week and not let them out of sight.

"I was so afraid. He kept tying me to beds, but he didn't do anything except hit me. I thought he was going to rape me when he tied me in an upstairs room, the one with the built-in closet. He left me there gagged and blindfolded. I didn't know where he was until all of sudden he started yelling something like, 'No. No. You're not real! Get away from me!' Then he was screaming and running down the steps. Next thing I knew, Jake and Ben were taking the blindfold and gag off me."

Adam knew Cynthia was going to recover from her ordeal, but she needed her family to help her heal. She had a whole new life to begin and seemed ready to get on with it, as if Wilbur's violence had thrust her through the portals to the future. He also realized she was right about him. It was time he went home, not knowing what would happen when he got there. He didn't know if he could repair his dysfunctional marriage, and he wasn't sure he wanted to. Letting Cynthia go was going to hurt. Their affair had really gotten to him.

"I'm going to miss you when you're with your kids," he whispered.

"And I'll miss you. But so does your wife. You need to call and tell her what happened. She'll probably want to drive over and be with you." Lifting her face to kiss him for what he knew would be the last time, she spoke softly before their lips met, "You know I will never say anything or let anyone hurt you or your family. You were my Great Affair. I couldn't have had a better one. Thank you."

When Adam walked into the kitchen, the others had found chairs around the yellow Formica table. Joe had refused to go to the hospital until he'd heard Autie's story, Jake and Ben had carried the recliner in to the kitchen so he could join the group.

Autie was sitting in an overstuffed chair their mother had favored, a cold beer pressed against his forehead. Yesterday they had been enemies, part of an eighty-year-old family feud. Today they accepted him as their long lost uncle.

Everybody was waiting for Adam. Since he had discovered the skeletons, he had the honor, or the duty, of finishing what he had started. In acknowledgment, Jake offered him a chair at the head of the table. As he sat down, everyone quit talking and looked at him as if he were a wise old seer.

"Autie," Adam began. "We are your grandnephews, George and Sarah's grandchildren - Donald's children. That's Jacob, the oldest. He took over the farm from Dad and worked it until he made big money from a side insurance business.

"I'm Adam. The second born. I live in Colorado and taught history at a college until I retired. I guess you know that I found the bodies and Sarah's journals.

"Benjamin there, he was a solider in Vietnam and now spends his time hunting and fishing. Makes his living as a substitute schoolteacher, but I think that's only in his spare time."

"Yeah, and I'm in a hurry to get back. Walleyes are running at Big Mac, so get on with it." Ben's laughter caused everyone else to lighten up and even brought a smile to Autie who asked him if there was room for one more fisherman in the boat.

"And the baby of the family. That's Joseph," Adam said, pointing at his brother who was obviously in great pain. "He's a big shot engineer in Texas, only person I know who earns a living producing the raw materials of fertilizer. We've always thought he was the king of the manure business, but he says it's not true.

"And you know who Cynthia is. She's the curator of the Medicine Lodge Historical Museum."

The old house had turned quiet again, the silence overwhelming, as if even the boards, nails, and plaster were straining to hear what Autie said. Nobody spoke, looked away, or even popped a top on a beer. The Roberts brothers and Cynthia stared at Autie, waiting for him to speak, gathered as if they were disciples at Christ's feet.

When he finally did, the Old West was alive in his voice and inflections. "Well now, I 'spect y'all be wanting to hear my words. I s'pose y'all been speculating on what happened to yer family in the olden days. I 'spect I'll tell. Been wanting to unload this story. Never could till now. I'll make a clean break of it. But I'm an old man, and I got to get me some promises first. I pertected some secrets and people fer too long to be shouting it out now."

"I believe we are aware of some of your concerns," Adam answered. "Please know that none of us, including Cynthia, has any interest in causing you any embarrassment or in bringing any undue notoriety to our family. We want to know the truth, if you know, and we think you do, about the murders of Consuelo and Jesus Vargas, and what happened in the storm cellar all those years ago.

"What promises do you want?"

Nobody in the room took their eyes off the centenarian, and to his credit he didn't flinch or back off. He had given back as good as he had gotten for over one hundred years, and he wasn't going to change now.

Stomping his cane on the linoleum floor and clearing his throat, the old man lost his composure, waiting to regain it before he spoke. "I be wanting my boy, Wilbur. No police! No jail! He goes with me. I'll take care of him. I know he's been in a heap of trouble, but he's all I got and I 'spect I'm all he's got. The two of us 're just gonna have to manage."

Joe was first to speak. "Sorry, but I can't vote for that. I vote that he goes to jail for many years. He tried to kill me and would have if you guys hadn't come along. I don't want to let him off. I've got surgery and a hospital stay coming. Turning that animal loose would be crazy. We will all bear the responsibility when he kills or rapes again."

The other brothers turned to Cynthia, knowing Joe would agree with what they decided, but Cynthia wasn't a member of their family and Wilbur had assaulted, tortured, and humiliated her. It was her call.

"I don't care," she said coldly. "He didn't rape me, and the bruises will heal. I'm strong enough to get past this. But I have a condition of my own. If he goes free, he can't stay around here. He's been stalking me for years. If I see him on the street after this, I'm calling the police."

"I don't think you're going to have to worry about him, at least not for a month of Sundays," Ben broke in. "He's tied up against one of the trees in the back. Crying, moaning, and sputtering about ghosts, old women, and knives. Begged me not to put him in the house, or any building for that matter. Says he can't go inside, they're waiting for him. I figure he saw Adam's ghosts."

"Count me in as a believer. I saw them too," Joe interrupted, a surge of pain forcing him to speak through clenched teeth. "They are as real as we are. Adam's right. Sarah is here, probably watching us right now, and she was no killer. She didn't do it."

"I know," Cynthia added. "Sarah, Jesus, and Consuelo all came to comfort me when that pig was . . . well, he was . . . it was awful. They're wonderful. Sarah wasn't a killer."

Speaking up quickly to hold off the comments he could see Jake planning and to get back to Autie's story, Adam rapped his now empty bottle on the table. He assured Joe and Cynthia everybody wanted to hear what they had seen, but they needed to finish with their elderly uncle first. "What about it?" he asked Autie. "Can you take Wilbur somewhere and keep him away from here? Sounds like a big job, especially in his condition. At your age, do you think you can handle it?"

"Before you answer that, Autie," Ben said with a faraway look in his eyes. "I saw cases just like Wilbur's in Nam - a friend of mine for one. Took a burst of automatic fire that shredded his clothes. Blew all his gear off without touching his body. It was impossible to have happened, but it did. He didn't have a wound or a break in his skin. He just stood there, damn near naked, looking up to the sky with shock in his eyes.

"As far as I know, he's still in a VA hospital. He's never recovered and he not going to. I don't think Wilbur will either. Just like my friend, he's growing worse by the minute. He's in much worse shape now than when you brought him back here.

"I'm no shrink, but as I've said, I've seen this before. He's going to need cared for as an infant for the rest of his life. Whatever he saw, or thought he saw, was too much for him. Scrambled his brains. I'll tell you, the light is on but nobody's home in that boy. I doubt he will ever be the same again."

Looking at each one of them in turn, making sure they all saw the determination in the winkled, hardened old features, Autie answered without hedging. "Yep, I can handle it just fine, fer as much time as I have left. Course y'all be a-knowing I've outlived my time and every morning I wake up breathing is a fanciful surprise.

"Howsomever, I got to be taking care of my boy. I know he ain't right. Sometimes, I swear that whole side of kin took more after Ma than anybody else.

"I be going back to the ranch in West Texas. Already decided. Owner has a cabin fer me and Wilbur along a crick, long ways from anywhere. More'n thirty miles across snakes, cactus, rocks, and desert to nowhere. It's just like living in the old days, that's why I be wanting to go there. No 'lectricity, no cars or trucks, and no people. It be living alone, like I always did.

"I reckon when I die, if the boy is like you say, and he stays that away, he'll go too. A fitting end fer my bunch, ain't it?

"The foreman is an old pard of mine, and he'll do what I ask. I'll be telling him all about Wilbur - iff'n he ain't getting no better - and ask him to make it an easy death fer him. He'll let my boy die when I'm gone. Reckon he won't have to do nothing if what Ben says be true but make him comfortable and let him go. He'll just go to sleep. My friend'll do it fer me. We been through some big doings together.

"I want my boy to go nice and peaceful and all. No pain. No suffering. Just let him die warm, and bury him in the same grave with me. Right next to the crick. We'll be wanting no headboards. No markers."

"Joe, what do you think," Ben asked, urging him with his voice and body language to agree. "I'll stake anything we got that Wilbur's gone for good. There's no way he'll ever be able to live alone. When Autie goes, he'll probably die within hours."

Everyone sat quietly as Joe, grimacing from the pain, tried to gather his thoughts. "He didn't break my leg. I did it falling off the porch. He wasn't successful killing me, so I suppose I should try to find some mercy for him, especially if he's brain-dead. Go ahead. But if I ever see him again, if he ever gets off that ranch and I know about it, I'll go after him with a gun."

They all wanted to believe that Wilbur would never bother anyone again. In fact, Adam wanted to think that when Autie died in a lonely cabin on a west Texas creek Wilbur wouldn't be far behind. Autie was right; it would be a fitting end. Adam told the old man they agreed on the condition that someone from the ranch escort them out to the cabin.

The old man asked for a glass of water with just a little whiskey, "need to wet my whistle," he said. Then he told his story. He began with tales he'd heard as a young child about his big brother, George, who'd disappeared one night with the gang's best horse.

Autie's description of life on the run transfixed his great-nephews. They wept with him as tears poured down his cheeks when he told them of his father's death at the hand of cowhands in Wyoming. His face crinkled into a smile as he related how he'd burned the barn and bunkhouse of the vigilantes responsible, and of his exciting but lonely ride from Wyoming to South Dakota as a ten-year-old.

His was a story that western movies should be made of and, at that moment, they were proud he was their uncle. He didn't sound like a man who would murder two young Californians huddling together in the dark. His listeners pulled their chairs closer as he told them of finding the brother he had never known and how proud he had been to be George's brother.

Without his father, he had felt lost. Maybe if his Pa had lived longer he could have resisted his mother's return to the outlaw ways, but she had promised a mother's love as well as money and fast horses.

The day they left George's ranch had been the worst of his life. "It were the most terrible," he said. "Worse even than watching Pa swing because I were so much in love with Consuelo. She was the purtiest gal I'd ever laid eyes on. Such long black hair. Her eyes lit up in the dark, and I could even come close to touching my fingers and thumbs around her waist.

"I knew she were meant fer me, that we'd have a life together and our own place. Fact is I started running with ma and her bunch so's I could get me some money fer stock. Consuelo hadn't said she'd marry up with me yet, but I thought it were just a matter of time. I never quit loving thet little gal. I'll take memories of her with me when I die.

"I 'spect it's my fault they got theirselves kilt, mostly on account of thet boy. Now he was a dandy, looked and acted just like her. Couldn't tell them apart." Eyes misting, the old man paused and looked out the window across the prairie before continuing.

"You know, the Sioux up in Dakota. They had 'em living in their tribe. Respected 'em too. Called 'em *berdache*, men living as women. *Boy-girls* we said in the old days. They was no big deal amongst the Indians, considered women in every way. They usually married and lived as another wife. Respected members of the tribe. Some thought they had special medicine powers. I kind of thought Jesus be one, only he couldn't dress like a woman around white folk. I didn't pay him no never-mind.

"One day out in thet ol' chicken house there, when he were picking up eggs, I asked him to have Consuelo meet me at night out by the wallow near the cottonwood George planted and Earl burnt down. He burnt it out of sheer meanness. I didn't wish him to set it afire.

"Don'tcha see? I had to tell her how much I loved her. She were the love of my life. I wanted to hold her and promise her the world. Well, shortly after sundown she came out. Leastways I thought it were her. Everything went as I planned, 'cept she wouldn't let me touch her, but she'd told me she loved me, and I were happy.

"We met again a couple of days later in the barn loft, but as she left, she fell and hurt herself. Then I saw her in the bright light, and saw I'd been played fer a fool. It weren't Consuelo at all, but her brother, the berdache.

"Now I had nothing against him being one, but I weren't like him, and people around town weren't so friendly to them that were. The Sioux, I guess they understood some stuff white folks didn't, but I were done as a cowboy and a good man if word of my meeting Jesus ever got around. It'd plumb ruint me, even if I told folks the truth thet he played me fer a fool. Nobody woulda believed me.

"I guess it near ruint my life anyhow. I figured Consuelo were in on it and were laughing at me. So's I told her and Jesus if they ever told anyone about it, I'd kill 'em. I was young and full of hate, and I 'spect I could have done it back then. I were never the same after that, like it'd taken my spirit away. Only seventeen and my heart broke by a woman who sent her brother out to whore with me.

"I were scared people'd find out, like they could just look at me and see what I done. I had to leave and head fer Texas. I were still afraid someone would find out, and I be hoping to get lost down on one of them big ranches. I 'spect I did. Never been back this way. Left two days after the murders and that's fact."

The room was silent as Autie stood and shuffled into the bathroom. The brothers and Cynthia exchanged glances as Jake handed around full bottles, but no one spoke. They were afraid they would break the spell.

"Well, I 'spect you be wanting to hear how they was kilt," he told them when he returned, his voice weary, the strain and exertion almost too much. "I already done told you it were my fault, and I've lived in hell ever since, knowing it were me that got the woman I loved kilt. You see, I still loved her - reckon I do to this day. Maybe sometime soon I'll finally get a chance to tell her.

"It were my fault 'cause I knew this bunch of fools around here were starting to wear hoods and sheets and act like they were gonna save America. Damn fools. Just a bunch of over-churched, led around by their wives, afeared their peckers would get them in trouble, poor-thinking fools. Against anyone and anything that didn't look and act like them and their nose-in-the-sky women.

"Shut down gambling, the pool hall, the whorehouse, and even tried to close the saloons. Feared a bunch of coloreds and Mexicans, maybe even Italians, were gonna come here and steal their daughters and their land. They'd go to meetings and brag 'bout how tough they be. I figured they were most afeared something tempting would lead 'em astray, but maybe that were just me.

"So I went to a meeting one time when my uncle be there. Fer some reason, he hated yer grandpa. Anyways, I started telling him and a few others that Jesus were nothing but a dirty, Mexican queer and his sister a whore, offering it free to everybody 'cept fer God-fearing white men.

It weren't long after that the Klan decided to send 'em back to California or kill 'em. The members were split over that decision. I convinced them sheet-wearers to spare their lives and send them back where they come from. Said it would be a lot worse fer the Mexican nation to have to live with them. Anyhow, that's why them white-sheeted fools turned up here one day.

"It were a real hot day, a storm coming in on the horizon. I remember it like it were yesterday. Your grandpa held them off with his rifle. I were proud of him. He were by far the best and bravest man there. When he put a bullet into a steam car and the horses went loco and stampeded, it were all over. I watched the whole shebang from the barn, knowing it were my fault the Klan came a calling. I had to make sure Consuelo was safe. I was thinking if I showed up to help, she would finally fall fer me. Being her pertecter and all.

"When the stock stampeded, I run across from the barn to the house and saw the killer running away. She'd done something terrible. It were plain as day. She run up the basement steps covered with blood. Almost knocked me over as she ran out the door. I only ever saw her once more in my life.

"Right then I heard Sarah screaming, and I run down to the basement and into the cellar. So dark I couldn't see nothing, but the killer had left a lamp burning by the stairs where she dropped it. I ran and picked it up and hurried back. It were terrible to see, worst I ever did. Sarah was a crying and a screaming, a big knife on the floor in front of her. My poor Consuelo and her scheming brother a-laying there in a big pool of blood. They'd been hacked to pieces. The girl I loved had been butchered, and I'd let her killer run away.

"So many times I wished I'd stayed, been brave like yer grandpa and told people what happened and who done it. But I couldn't. She knew the story, I'd told her one time, hoping she would help 'cause I were feeling so bad, but she only laughed and called me a terrible name I won't even tell. I knew she'd tell the whole story if she were caught, so I lit out fer Texas."

"Autie," Cynthia said softly when the old man stopped to gasp for air. "I think you saw, Molly, your mother. Didn't you? It was your mother who killed Consuelo and Jesus. Wasn't it?"

The old man managed one more sip of his whiskey and water. "Yes'm. My own ma murdered the girl I loved. I always figgered she did it to spite George. She was always going on 'bout how her son turned away from her on account of Sarah. He was too uppity fer his own good, she said, and he needed to be brought down. But Ma were just mean - filled with a bad spirit. She mighta just done it out of meanness, 'cause it were the best way to hurt George or even me. I come to realize much later that she always blamed me fer Pa's death, thought if I'd done better he'd a still been alive.

"I laid eyes on her fer the last time as I were riding out of town fer Texas. She were so drunk she didn't know it were me. Lying there in the mud back of the saloon, trying to get men to lay with her for a drink."

CHAPTER TWENTY-FOUR

AFTER AUTIE FINISHED HIS STORY, THEY WALKED WITH HIM to the charred stump of the cottonwood. For eighty years, the huge tree had stood silent watch as the prairie transformed from sprawling cattle ranches to wheat farms. Cotton had fallen from its branches in blizzards of white across the backs of cattle driven from the southwestern deserts and onto gleaming metal machines chewing giant swaths through acres of golden wheat.

For a few hours, the giant of the prairie had served as a monument to the only woman Autie had ever loved, and then an eighty-year-old feud spawned by fear and hatred had destroyed it.

There wasn't a dry eye in the bunch as the old man fell to his knees caressing the earth covering Consuelo's grave. He was still crying about being responsible for the death of the only woman he had ever loved as he shuffled back to the house, refusing offers of help and support.

Adam had wanted Consuelo, Jesus, and Sarah to appear and assure the old man they were well and happy - even hoping the beautiful dark-haired California woman would tell the old man of her great love for him. But it was not to be.

The Roberts brothers closed up the old house and everyone began going their separate ways. Cynthia gave hugs to each of them and told them not to be strangers. She helped Autie into the backseat of Sue's SUV while Ben and Jake placed the trussed, terrified, and moaning Wilbur on the other side of the backseat. After Cynthia got into the front seat, Sue drove away. Before going to see her family, she and Sue were driving to the small county airport where Autie and Wilbur would meet the ranch owner's private plane.

Jake and Ben hustled to get ready to take Joe to the hospital, hoping there would still be time for eighteen holes after they left him. None of the brothers had ever believed in long goodbyes and weren't about to start anytime soon. Adam managed, however, to steal a few minutes alone with Joe while Ben and Jake boarded-up the old house.

"Joe," he asked quietly. "I have to know. Did your cameras get any pictures of the spirits? It's important to me. I think they're here, but I fought against the idea so much as a child trying to get over being afraid, I still can't let myself accept the notion ghosts might actually be real. If the cameras don't prove it, I may never find any peace. Did you look? What did you see?"

"Sorry, big Brother," the injured man whispered hoarsely as another spasm of pain shook his body. "After I saw Grandma, I knew she was real, and I didn't want anybody or anything doubting or proving she wasn't. If the camera recorded her, I didn't want her spirit commercialized.

"I deleted everything in the camera without looking, just about the time the sun came up. I know in my heart they are here. They spoke to me, and that's all I need to know. You need to believe in them too, now tell those two to get me to the hospital."

Adam and Jake loaded Joe into the car just after Jake told Joe he was the weird one in the family. At least, according to their older brother, Adam always wanted to believe he saw ghosts only in dreams, but Joe saw them when he was awake and that made him a real space cadet. "Yeah. Move to Boulder with Adam and the other tree-huggers," Ben said as he started the car.

As he drove slowly away from the old farmhouse, Adam supposed Jake would live his entire life without ever admitting the possibility that the spirits of those who had gone before were still with them.

Joe would always believe he saw his grandmother and received her blessing. For the rest of his life, he would insist she saved him by appearing before Wilbur. He may forget his burial in Consuelo and Jesus' tomb, but he would always remember the love on Sarah's face.

As for himself, he still couldn't find any answers. He didn't know if Consuelo, Jesus, Sarah, and Molly appeared before him as spirits or if they only existed in his dreams. He imagined the woman with the knife who kept him awake as a child was Molly. But was she a ghost, or a figment of his imagination based on a horrible act his father had witnessed as a frightened seven-year-old boy?

He hoped that the spirits were real and that the other three forgave Molly, that they reunited with the rest of their family, and that they all enjoyed the endless prairies of their youth in peace. Adam also figured, however, if they were now free to walk into the light and pass on to the other side, Molly might go to a distinctly hotter place.

During the three-hour drive from the old farmhouse to Boulder, Adam needed to decide what to tell his wife. He didn't know if he would tell her about Cynthia. His marriage might end if he told her the truth, but it also might be over if he didn't.

As Adam drove through Medicine Lodge, the dilemma was a burden. He couldn't decide and knew he must. As he turned onto the Interstate into Colorado, his anxiety lost its urgency. Soon, the towering peaks of the Rockies sparkled in the afternoon sun, and he thought about the cool, clear mountain lakes high in the lofty crags. Snow would fall on them before long, and another ski season of Colorado powder would begin.

If he was lucky, there would be steak for the grill when he got home, and an iced pitcher of something cool and refreshing for dinner - the wonderful libation his wife, the scientist, mixed. He would tell her he loved her. *'Perhaps saying it,'* he thought, *'will make it true.'*

Cynthia joined Sarah, Jesus, Consuelo, Cowboy George, and Autie in his past. He would try to live with her being his one great secret.

Adam hoped to see the spirits of his youth again, but knew he probably would not. He was truly richer for having known them - maybe he always had been.

Printed in the United States
44833LVS00002B/205-306